The
DRAGON
of YNYS

The
DRAGON
of YNYS

Minerva Cerridwen

Detroit, Michigan

The Dragon of Ynys

Editorial Services by E.D.E. Bell

Cover Illustration
Copyright © 2020 Ulla Thynell
ullathynell.com

Interior Design by G.C. Bell

Published by Atthis Arts, LLC
Detroit, Michigan
atthisarts.com

ISBN 978-1-945009-68-6

Library of Congress Control Number: 2020943942

Content Notes:

This fairy tale contains instances of trans-antagonism and flirting to an aro ace character. Both are addressed on-page and resolved. The dragon conducts off-page, non-violent theft. The book contains visuals of spiders and an off-page avalanche.

Chapter One

There were many fields between the village of Ynys and the nearest city in the south. To the north and west, a mountain chain separated Ynys from the rest of the world, and to the east streamed a wide river. The only merchants who ever reached the village were those who passed by boat. As there weren't any regular markets, the villagers had to provide for themselves. Most of them were hard-working farmers and craftsmen, millers and weavers, butchers and bakers.

Everyone knew each other in Ynys, and meeting a new person was an event people might talk about for years. So when an unkempt middle-aged man with a stammer came from the mountains, wearing clothes that had gone out of fashion in the village years ago, it didn't take long before the whispers began. They said he'd started working for one of the millers and lived at his house. That his name was Heath and that he had once lived in Ynys, but that he'd left as a teenager. There were many theories about the why and how, but no one seemed to remember him, so most people believed he really came from far away and spread the rumours himself, thinking that the villagers would be more inclined to let him stay if they thought this was his hometown. According to those who'd taken the time to talk with him, he was full of all sorts of fantastical and amusing tales, so coming up with one about himself wouldn't have been much of a stretch. Secret societies, whispering spiders, the eerie chime of ghostly songs on the wind in the mountains; nothing was too far-fetched for this man.

At any other time, such an intriguing break from what was considered normal life in Ynys would have earned months of gossip. Yet Heath had only lived there for five days when there was something even more important on the villagers' minds. The mayor's golden chain had gone missing.

The mayor was not a young person anymore, so at first the more youthful villagers concluded she'd merely put the chain somewhere out of the ordinary and forgotten about it. But after searching her house and garden, it was clear: it must have been a theft.

Immediately, fingers were pointing at the new-comer. He claimed that he hadn't even been aware that the mayor owned a chain and that he'd only come here to start a new life, but no one listened to him. Nobody in the village was known to be a thief, so it had to be him. But the mayor would not accuse anyone without proof and called in the help of the local knight to launch an investigation.

This stocky young man had spent the past year by the side of Lady Edelweiss, the old knight who was respected by everyone for her adventures throughout the kingdom. Visiting places other than Ynys was extraordinary in itself, but she had met an actual king and known him long enough to be knighted.

Now, however, she was retired and Sir Violet was on his own to handle the village's knightly business. Considering that Ynys was too small for anyone to try and besiege it—if they'd bother to make the long journey at all—Violet's job so far had consisted of solving neighbourly fights and finding miss-ing handkerchiefs. Nothing that involved both the mayor *and* gold and would make the whole village follow his every move. But he felt at ease when he came to the mayor's house. Determined to handle this as he would any other case, he asked to see the garden.

Nothing was broken or bent. The earth had been trampled by those who had been looking for the chain, so he doubted he'd find a trace that would lead to the thief, even if he could have remembered Lady Edelweiss' many lessons about footprints. In all fairness, he had never paid much attention to them.

But then he almost stumbled. And as he stood back and looked at the ground, he saw that the soil was depressed over an area wider than his legs were long. The impression had the shape of a large paw and there were claw marks. It wouldn't have taken many lessons to know that there was only one creature that could leave a print like that.

Violet had heard quite a few stories about dragons and while they didn't agree on most points, all of them mentioned that their kind preferred to live in caves. So without wasting time, he informed the mayor that he had found a clue, and then left her house and the village. He walked all the way to the mountainside and it took no longer than an hour to find a large cave.

As he entered, he wished the dragon had chosen

a sunnier day. Cloudy as it was, he could only see a couple of steps ahead, and the darkness beyond made it impossible to know how deep into the rock the cavity went.

He trod onto what felt like thick carpet, and grunted as he stubbed his toe against something hard. A similar growl sounded in answer. For a moment, Violet wondered if echoes could be louder than the original sound, but then there was a rustle and the tinkling of metal against metal.

"Excuse me?" he called.

A black mass moved out of the darkness and two yellow eyes fixed on Violet. "Excuse me, you said?" a deep, reverberating voice asked. "What should I excuse you for?"

"Er . . ." Violet took a few steps back from the giant, scaly face. "Disturbing you, I suppose. Though actually, I guess that you are the one who owes the mayor an apology."

"An apology?" the dragon repeated. "We are meeting for the first time and you are demanding an apology? Is that how your people say hello?" The creature sat on its hind legs, but its head still towered high above Violet's. It did catch more light now, and he could see the gleam of enormous fangs.

He wondered if this had been a safe plan, but then decided it would be better to just press on. "Fine," he said, "I don't care all that much about the apology. But what I do care about is that the mayor employed me to return her golden chain. I have reason to believe it is in your possession, and I would like to take it back."

"Oh, all right." The dragon sounded rather amused. "I suppose that in a place like your village, that chain really is the only perk of being mayor. Far be it from me to take that joy away."

With a loud tinkle of moving coins, the beast shifted and reached behind itself. Then it dangled the golden chain, hooked on a claw that looked at least as dangerous as the fangs, in front of Violet's face.

"Here you go. Sorry for causing you trouble."

"Thank you." Violet was not exactly an expert when it came to gold, but the chain seemed to be unharmed. "I will leave you to it, then."

"To what?"

"To . . . being a dragon and doing . . . dragon things." Violet frowned. "What I meant is, I'll be off, returning this."

"Of course. Have a nice day." Going by the shimmer of its teeth, the dragon was still smiling.

With the chain safely back around the mayor's neck, a council meeting was called in order to decide what to do about the dragon.

"I don't think there is much you *can* do about it," Violet mused. "I've seen it, and I think it's a little too heavy to simply kick out of its lair. Besides, it's not actually in our village. And it was quite polite."

"But surely a dragon can mean nothing but trouble," one of the two council members piped up. "Perhaps this was only the beginning!"

"We don't know how long this dragon has been living here," the mayor countered. "We've never even seen it fly over Ynys. At least I haven't. Now it has stolen one thing and returned it upon a simple request from Sir Violet. I don't think we have to fear this creature."

So, to Violet's relief, the meeting was over before dinnertime, and the mayor did not assign the village's only knight to go up against the dragon.

In fact, from that point on, Violet's work became even easier than it had been before.

The next time something went missing was a few

months later, and Violet had almost forgotten about the beast. He went through all the usual motions before he thought of visiting the cave, and indeed found the old woman's ring there.

After that, the thefts started happening more and more frequently, as apparently the dragon grew increasingly bored. Every time an object went missing, Violet would find it in the same place. Sometimes it required a long argument, but he always managed to return the loot to its owner. In the end, Violet was visiting the dragon every week, and villagers sometimes even forgot to mention *what* they were missing before they sent him to the cave.

The only time he was at a loss was about three years after first discovering the dragon. The item he was supposed to find was the shoemaker's wedding dress. So far, the dragon had only ever stolen gems and pieces of jewellery, except for a few worthless shiny buttons and knives. But a dress would not gleam in the sunlight. Especially not if it had neatly been stored in a wardrobe, like the shoemaker explained.

Still, Violet didn't find it at any of the suspects' homes and his investigation came to a dead end. He felt very silly as he walked the now familiar path to the cave, muttering to himself that a dragon couldn't possibly open a wardrobe with its claws.

But when he entered the lair, his assumptions were proved wrong. There was the dress, displayed on a vaguely human-shaped pile of silver goblets, in a prime spot at the front of the mountain of treasures where it caught the light from the entrance.

"Seriously?" Violet stared at the dragon. "It's not even shiny!"

"It is," the dragon replied, looking slightly indignant. "Don't you see all these fine pearls woven into the fabric?" It gently, almost tenderly, ticked a claw against one of them. "And even without those, it would be a work of art. Can't you see the quality of the silk? How remarkably the skirt has been cut? This dress is definitely worth hoarding."

"The actual owner probably agrees," Violet pointed out, crossing his arms as he looked up at the dragon.

"Are you sure?" the creature asked. "Are you certain that the owner appreciates its beauty as much as I do?"

Rolling his eyes, Violet lifted the dress off its improvised mannequin and stomped back to the village.

Only a few weeks later, he was visited by the carpenter.

"Dear Master Spruce, where are your trousers?" Violet asked as he opened the door to see the middle-aged man standing there in his breeches.

"That's what I'm employin' you for, isn't it? To find out where my bloomin' trousers are?"

It turned out that the old Master had gone for a swim in a quiet part of the river, and when he returned, the garment had disappeared. He had first accused his friends of the prank, but they denied knowing that he'd gone swimming at all, and here he was, still trouserless.

"So what's so beautiful about these?" Violet asked the dragon, leaning against the cave wall as he waited for the beast to untie the trousers from the ceiling's stalactites.

"Oh, nothing, really," it replied with an unsettlingly wide grin. "This was just funny."

Thus, life in Ynys bumbled on as it always had, but with a little more cursing as people found that one of their belongings had not-so-mysteriously disappeared again. Heath was still working at the mill, no longer accused of everything and anything out of the ordinary; the dragon seemed to amuse itself, and Violet got more physical exercise than he liked, making the long walk to the cave and back so often.

It had been about ten years since his first meeting with the dragon when he entered the bakery on a fine morning.

Juniper was, in Violet's opinion, the best baker in the village. She bought the most delicious spices from the merchants when they sailed past, and he had never disliked any of her pastries. But his absolute favourites, which he came to buy here every morning for breakfast, were the cinnamon rolls.

Today, however, the shop was empty.

There was no bread, so freshly baked that he could almost hear the crisp of its crust as it lay in the racks, no pies with a succulent filling of cherries or berries, none of the sweet biscuits the children were so fond of. And most importantly, no cinnamon rolls.

"Hello?" Violet called, standing on tiptoes, as though the extra height would help him see into the darkness at the back of the shop. "Anyone home?"

There were distant footsteps and the sound of doors opening and closing, before the baker's wife appeared from the back room, almost at a run.

"Sir Violet!" she exclaimed. "I was just on my way to find you!"

"I'm not later than other mornings, am I?" Violet asked. "Nor earlier. How come the shop is so empty, Holly?"

The tall woman bit her lip. "Sir . . . it's Juniper. She is missing."

"Missing?" Violet repeated incredulously. "She was here yesterday!"

Holly sighed. "Yes. She was here then. She even came to bed last night. But when I woke up this morning, she was gone."

"Maybe she went for a morning stroll," Violet suggested. "It can't be easy, filling a bakery every single day. Surely she needs some fresh air now and then. You know what, I'll just come back later for my breakfast."

"Your breakfast? Really? That's what's on your mind right now?" Holly shook her head. "This is serious. I know Juniper better than anyone. Do you think I'd be panicking if I thought she was just taking a walk? She's been gone for hours!"

Violet frowned and studied her expression. "You're panicking? I mean, I thought you were just . . . mentioning this."

He wasn't prepared for the way Holly's shoulders slumped and her serious expression yielded to despair. She was always composed, always politely cheerful, even on mornings when she must have heard the same witty remark about the weather several times already before Violet greeted her with it.

"Please. You must find her," she said, her voice trembling slightly.

"Find her?" Violet repeated, realisation dawning on him. "Oh . . . That monster! So now even jewels and clothes aren't enough anymore!"

"What are you talking about?"

Violet straightened up and gave Holly a nod. "Don't you worry. I'll bring your wife back within three hours at most!"

"But . . . I don't think . . . "

Violet didn't stay to listen. If he was to make the

long walk this early in the day, without any breakfast, he wanted it over with as soon as possible. He
only made a quick stop at home to pick up his sword.

"Dragon!" he roared as he entered the lair, wiping
the sweat off his forehead before drawing the weapon.
Carrying its weight had made the walk so much
harder. "I don't know what you're playing at this
time, but you've gone too far!"

"Ugh . . ." came the answer from deep inside
the cave, "I haven't gone anywhere. Do you have
any idea how early it is?"

"I don't crumbling care, you foul beast. You stay
away from humans! They aren't yours to hoard!"

"Humans?" With its familiar rustle and tinkle,
the dragon moved until it was almost nose to nose
with Violet. "Why would I hoard *humans*?"

"Oh, don't act like there's ever anything that
goes missing and doesn't show up in your cosy little
cave. I know you did it. Now tell me, where are you
hiding her?" Violet looked around and even glanced
at the ceiling, but there was no immediate trace of a
woman in her forties with flour on her apron.

"I have no idea what you are talking about," the dragon said. "Your presumption is ridiculous. Hoarding your kind? Have you seen yourself? I hoard *beautiful* things. No weird, bald, scale-less bipeds . . ."

"Except if you got bored again," Violet said, unimpressed by the insults. Of course the dragon would try to distract him if it really was guilty. But Violet wouldn't let it. He was a professional, special-ised in dragon crimes. *This* dragon's crimes. "I bet you fancied a change. Wanted something that wasn't so straining on the eye. Even dragon eyes must get old and tired. Or maybe you wanted something that talks back. After all this time in here, you must have gotten awfully lonely."

The dragon snorted. "How could I get lonely when I have you constantly swooping into my home?"

"I'll tell you this," Violet said, pointing his sword at the dragon's scaly face. "If you start harming us, if you start hurting humans, you can say goodbye to your peaceful existence. The whole village will be crowding your space with pitchforks and skewers."

"Oh dear," the dragon sighed, leaning back. "You must care an awful lot about her."

"She is a fellow citizen of Ynys and I have been employed to find her."

"Well, I hope you do, and soon. You're no fun at all in this mood. But be my guest. Search the whole cave if you really must. But I can save you the trouble and tell you that she is not here. I do not hoard anything or anyone that needs feeding. Ever. Not just because I would be keeping them against their will, but also because it's more trouble than it's worth. And before you think of spawning that next accusation that's forming in your deteriorated little brain: no. I did not eat her." The creature's nostrils widened and for the first time in ten years, Violet wondered if he should be afraid of it.

Then it turned around and retreated to its usual resting spot.

Violet sheathed his sword and picked up some handfuls of coins and necklaces. He even dragged a large harness from the pile of treasure, but he felt utterly ridiculous. *If* Juniper were here, that would mean she was either buried under the hoard, or so good at keeping still in the shadows that it had to mean she did not want to be found.

And the dragon was right. After all these years, Violet should have realised that harming people was not its style. His detecting skills *had* deteriorated, but in his defence, that was the dragon's fault, being the only compulsive thief in the neighbourhood.

Now he didn't have a clue what to do.

"If you're not looking for her, why are you still here?" the dragon growled, not even opening its eyes.

"I'm . . . thinking," Violet answered.

"Ah. I understand why you want me to witness such an extraordinary moment."

Violet felt strangely relieved that the dragon still made the effort to reply.

"I don't know where else to look for Juniper," he confessed.

"Yes. I understood that, too. But I think I made it clear that I can't help you. I do not know this lady. I don't know where she was last seen, if someone might have a motive to attack her, if she could really be in danger. All I know is that I want to continue my nap."

"Of course," Violet said. "I'll . . . go back and question her wife. Find out all those things."

"You didn't already?" The dragon now opened one mocking, yellow eye. "You are a lousy knight. I hope that, in spite of your services, the lady will be found unharmed."

"Me too. Thanks," Violet muttered.

"One more thing," the dragon said as he made to leave. "I hope it's obvious that you are not to visit me this early ever again."

"No. Yeah. I'm not planning to."

"Good."

Chapter Two

It wasn't all hunger that gnawed at Violet's stomach on the way back to the bakery. He had been so certain that Juniper would be walking back with him. Holly would have thanked him, Juniper would have started baking, there would have been tarts at teatime. Now he almost wished that the dragon *did* kidnap people. At least he would have kept his promise to Holly then. He wouldn't have to go and confess that he wasn't a good knight at all.

If anything had happened to Juniper during the time he had wasted, Holly would rightfully hold him responsible, and he doubted she would calmly accept his excuses. Holly was always very kind, and more patient with old people who were figuring out the coins in their wallets than Violet himself could ever imagine being. But other times, when someone made an unfortunate or rude comment, she could look so stern that he felt a strange urge to go stand in the corner and never come out again, even though it wasn't directed at him. And the mistake *he* had just made was much worse than insinuating Juniper might be using the wrong sort of apple in her apple pie.

He was still debating how to best brace himself when he heard Holly's voice.

"Sir Violet?"

He turned around as slowly as he dared. "Holly. I thought I'd find you back at the bakery."

"I couldn't just sit there," she said, carefully opening the fence around Farmer Willow's grounds, making sure that the farmer's enthusiastically barking beagle stayed on the other side. "I went to see some friends and family, you know, just asking around. But . . . Juniper isn't with any of them."

"Yes. About that . . ." Violet cleared his throat. "I went to see the dragon. I mean, it does steal everything. So I thought, why not your wife, right?"

"Because she isn't a thing?" Holly suggested.

"Yes, well. Apparently the dragon thinks that's a sound reason, too. Long story short, she wasn't there."

"I didn't think she would be," Holly said, looking dejected. "I think she may have needed a moment alone. Or, well, without me. Because we had a row last night. I meant to tell you, but . . . you dashed off. I hoped maybe she'd have returned by now. But she's just . . . disappeared. And I'm worried."

"And you don't think any of the people you've talked to might be hiding her?" Violet asked.

"I think they all know that they could tell me if Juniper doesn't want to see me. They're worried, too."

"Surely you don't think anyone would want to hurt her?"

"No," Holly said. "Why would they? Because of a dry piece of cake?" She shook her head. "I think that maybe she *did* go for a walk, but it wouldn't be like her to stay out on her own this long. She gets bored when there's nothing to do, so I thought she might go and help out at the farm, but no . . . Maybe she stopped paying attention to where she was headed and got lost outside the village? I just can't imagine she wouldn't at least have told me if she was planning to stay out all day . . ."

"Yeah, and there's the bakery to think of," Violet agreed. "Even if it was a really bad row, surely she wouldn't just leave her duties behind."

"Well, it *was* a bad row." Holly sighed and sat

down on the low fence. Behind her, the dog was still sniffing around restlessly, but at least it had gone quiet. "I really want to talk it through with her, but after so many years I'm certain she knows she doesn't have to stay away if she needs time before we do that. Something is off, and I just want to make sure she's all right."

"Would you mind telling me what happened? Maybe it can give us a clue as to where she is," Violet said, thinking it would be the kind of question the dragon might ask.

Holly hesitated. "It's delicate. I'm not sure it's my story to tell."

"I'd love to hear Juniper's take instead, but then that would mean we'd found her already," Violet pointed out.

"That's not what I mean," Holly said. "I think that to understand what happened, I'd have to tell you something that's not really about me or Juniper. Sharing it with you might help to find her, but you have to promise me not to tell anyone else."

"Of course." Violet had been asked not to talk about some of the objects he'd had to retrieve from the dragon cave in the past, and he'd always kept his word. He definitely would now—it was clear how much this mattered to Holly, considering that she hesitated to tell him even though every bit of information could be useful in their search for Juniper. "Keeping secrets is in my code of honour," he assured her.

Holly studied his face for a moment and then nodded. "I'll start at the beginning then. My cousin, Moss . . . She visited yesterday in the early afternoon, as she does every week. Most of the time she's a little hurried because she lives on the other side of the village, but it's tradition that she comes in for a piece of cake, you know? So usually she sits down and eats, we talk about what we've been up to, and she's off again. But this time, she was all solemn and polite. There was clearly something on her mind, but she'd already finished her cake by the time she told me what it was. She wanted my advice about her youngest child, Lilac."

"Oh. I know him," Violet commented. "Very sweet kid."

"Yes. She is."

"She?"

"That's why I'm asking you to keep this to yourself. I haven't spoken to Lilac, so I don't know if she's ready for anyone else to know."

"You can trust me," Violet said earnestly, feeling that his pledge of secrecy had never been more important.

"Lilac has always shown more interest in her sisters' dolls than in any of her own toys. And when she's playing with her friends, she's made it very clear that she doesn't like being called a 'hero' or a 'prince', because she'd much rather be a heroic *princess*. This time, Moss had found out that she was playing outdoors in one of her sisters' dresses. She told Lilac that that was not a 'proper thing' to do for a boy."

"Wait," Violet said, "and she dared repeat that to you?"

Holly shrugged sadly. "Lilac answered that in that case, she'd much rather be a girl. And apparently there'd been other things, smaller things, that made Moss think Lilac might never have thought of herself as a boy. But she'd never said it outright. Now that she had, Moss felt she should do something, but she had no idea what. And so she came to me to ask how she was supposed to act. Because I'm the only one she knows who has experienced the same thing as Lilac."

"Okay . . . " Violet said. "I'm not quite sure where

you're going with this. I mean, the thing about the dress was unfortunate, but it's good that Moss came to you, right? How does Juniper fit into any of this?"

"Well, it would have been good if Moss had actually listened to me." Holly frowned. "It seemed that with everything I said about allowing Lilac to express herself, she became more convinced that she should protect her from being 'different'. She assured me that Lilac could be herself at home, but that to the rest of the village, it would be safer to pretend she was a boy until she's older. Because the world is not always a kind place and she has to be careful."

"She may have a point about the world, but as far as I know, pretending to be someone you're not has never really helped anyone," Violet remarked.

"Exactly. I can see where she's coming from, but having to hide would make Lilac feel as if there really *is* something wrong with her. Or at least as if her mother thinks there is. It would make it harder for Lilac to accept herself."

Violet nodded.

"But Moss just kept coming up with reasons not to follow my advice. Lilac is only six, so Moss fears that she may always be considered the 'odd one' because the other kids don't understand. And that if Lilac's gender identity is still evolving, they may laugh at her if it turns out that she's not a girl after all. But I honestly think Moss is making more problems than those kids ever would. I was even younger when I knew I was a girl, and being myself has never caused me unhappiness. Other people's reactions may not always have been ideal, but I was lucky to have parents who supported me and taught me to love myself the way I am. Without that kind of acceptance from my family, how would I have learned to stand up for myself? I would probably have felt too ashamed to react. I would have been hurt all the more by what people were saying, because I'd start believing they were right.

"But Moss didn't seem to understand. She kept suggesting ways Lilac could 'subtly' be herself. By the time she went home, I felt like I hadn't gotten through to her at all. Juniper had been in the bakery as long as we'd been talking, but when there was a lull between customers, I poured it all onto her. How I couldn't understand that this was still an issue, even for my own cousin, who's known me all her life. Who knows that while I did not live up to expectations, I have found happiness and love. And what I understood even less was that Moss would come to me, but decided not to listen.

"Juniper pointed out that Moss was only figuring out how to best protect her child. That she wanted Lilac to be safe at all costs.

"'Even at the cost of her own happiness?' I asked. Well, I suppose it was more like screaming. I couldn't believe what I was hearing. My own wife, agreeing that a child should hide who she really is?

"I became angry and said that I wished we were still in the old days of the stories, when people made heroic gestures rather than bending over backwards to avoid confrontations. That I wished there was a way to make everyone, all over the world, realise that there's nothing wrong with being different from what is believed to be the norm. And—" Holly's voice broke. "And that if even *she* didn't support me, a wish was all it would ever be."

Violet frowned and said nothing, giving Holly time to collect herself. The dog wasn't so polite and resumed barking vehemently at a shrub.

"We didn't really talk after that," Holly continued after a moment. "Juniper was shocked by my outburst and I was too upset to talk it out. As I calmed down, it became easier to remember that Juniper has always had my back, just as much as I've had hers. I know she wants the best for Lilac, too. She was probably trying to help me see things from Moss' perspective to reassure me that Lilac is safe, and not because she agrees with what Moss said. Neither might Moss, even—my cousin always explores every side of an argument and sometimes keeps arguing just to hear more thoughts on a particular subject and make sure she's looked at it from every angle. So I get why Juniper trusts that Moss will eventually make the right decisions for Lilac, but an analysis of my cousin's viewpoint really wasn't what I needed yesterday. I just needed Juniper to comfort me, and she didn't. But I didn't have the energy to tell her that, so I went to bed early and pretended to be asleep when she joined me."

"And then, in the morning, she was gone," Violet concluded.

"Yes." Holly winced. "I don't know what to do now. I wouldn't mind giving her space if I knew where she was, but . . . she's really vanished. She must have left the village and I'm worried something bad has happened to her." She pulled her dark red scarf more closely around her shoulders.

Violet guessed it soothed her, as the mere thought

of wearing a scarf in this season was enough to make him sweat. "What could happen to a genius baker like her? Surely she can handle anything," he said, trying to lighten things up a bit, but, if possible, Holly looked even more distraught.

"If we are going to look for her—" Violet started, but the dog was now so loud that his words were almost inaudible. "Will you *please* be quiet?"

Holly stood up and stepped over the fence to inspect the shrub. "What did you see, Elmo? Surely you're not saying Juniper is hiding in there?"

The attention seemed to calm Elmo, and Violet rolled his eyes at the dog's antics. "As I was saying, if we want to look for her outside the village, we probably need a bigger search party. We can't know which way she's gone, after all."

Holly was still staring at the dog. "What if he *can* smell her?"

"Er, that shrub is definitely too small for her," Violet commented.

"Not *here*." Holly gave him a look. "But what if he can smell her trail?" She unwound the scarf and offered it to the beagle. "Take a good sniff, Elmo. Where did she go?"

The dog just looked up at her and wagged his tail.

"I'm afraid he's not trained to do that." Farmer Willow had come out, probably to see what all the yapping was about. "His sense of smell is good enough, but I doubt he understands what you want from him."

Holly deflated and put the scarf back around her shoulders. "Do you know any dogs who *can* do it?"

Willow shrugged. "Not really. I'm sorry . . ."

Violet slowly looked from the dog to the scarf and back. "What about the dragon?"

"What?" Holly turned around sharply. "Didn't you just say you went to see it? And that she wasn't there? If that's not true, what have you been doing for more than two hours?"

"No. Not like that," Violet said, trying not to shrink in shame. "I mean: a dragon's sense of smell must be really good. Better than a dog's. After all, it can smell gold, and that's never had much of a scent to me."

"And do you think the dragon would help us?" Holly looked doubtful.

"Well, we could always ask. At least it will understand us. And surely it would be faster than searching the fields without direction."

Holly nodded. "We can leave right away. All we

need is something that smells like Juniper, right? And I've got her scarf right here."

"Yeah. If the dragon wants payment, we can arrange it later," Violet said. "My only condition is that I can pick up something to eat on the way there, because if I don't, I'm pretty sure I'll faint."

"Of c—"

Elmo distracted them all by finally diving into the shrub.

"Oh, it's that rat again." Willow chuckled fondly. "He keeps chasing it. I think they've secretly become friends." Then he turned to Holly. "If I see Juniper, I'll tell her you're looking for her, okay? But if she's somewhere out there, I hope you will find her soon and patch things up between you two."

"Thank you," Holly said softly, giving the farmer's arm a squeeze.

Chapter Three

"**B**ack again?" the dragon's voice greeted them. Holly looked around the cave. "Wow," she breathed. "You've gathered quite a hoard. I thought Sir Violet said he always returned everything that was stolen to the owners."

"I'm honoured that my collection impresses you," the dragon said, moving closer to study her. "I hoarded a lot of it before I moved here. But even now, most thefts haven't been detected."

"*Most* thefts?" Violet repeated indignantly.

"Of course. I'm quite good at picking things people won't miss at all. Stuff they no longer need. Actually, I'm doing them a favour, getting it out of their way." The dragon grinned.

"Right." Violet awkwardly cleared his throat, resolving to tell the villagers that they should check if anything was missing from their attics. "I hope you don't mind that I showed my friend where you live. Her name is Holly and she is Juniper's wife."

"The more the merrier," the dragon said. "At least as long as they aren't bringing pitchforks."

"Why would I do that?" Holly looked puzzled.

"Oh. It's just a little inside joke between me and our knight." The dragon leaned in even closer to her.

"All right," she said, letting it sniff her arm. "I'm pleased to meet you. Everyone in the village has, of course, heard about you. You once owned one of our baking trays for about twenty-four hours, if I remember it correctly."

"I hope I didn't cause any inconvenience," the dragon replied.

"We managed," she said. "At least you never attacked the boats. That would have caused a lot more trouble."

"Yes. I thought Ynys might depend on some of the goods they carry."

"Thank you for taking that into account." Holly gave him a grateful nod. "Would you mind me asking your name? I've always wondered."

The dragon's lips curled into a smile. "Now here's a question that our knight has not ever bothered to ask in ten years' time. Thank you, dear lady. My name is Snap."

"Just call me Holly. No need for a 'lady', or I'll feel like *I'm* a knight. How should I refer to you? He? She? They? Something else?"

"Just use 'he' and 'him'," the dragon answered, bending his head a little. "I'm liking you more and more."

"So you're serious? Sir Violet has never asked?"

Violet huffed. "It's not as if *Snap* has ever asked *my* name."

"Oh, but clearly you were too fond of your privacy to share it before you knew mine," Snap said. "Sir Violet, hmm? The last knight I encountered used the title of Knight, not Sir."

"Some do," Holly supplied. "But others use Sir, like Sir Violet, or Lady, like Lady Edelweiss."

"You don't actually need to call me 'Sir'," Violet mumbled. "No royal ever knighted me. Or met me, for that matter. People in Ynys only call me that because I do what they think knights do."

"Oh," the dragon said slowly. "So I may actually have hit a nerve earlier. You're not a lousy knight. You're not a knight at all!"

"Yes, thank you, I'm aware. That's why we're here, in fact. We need your help."

"My *help*?" Snap let out a short laugh. "Not so long ago, you were accusing me. You thought I might have eaten . . . Juniper, was it?"

Holly stared at Violet. "Did you really think that?"

"No, that's an assumption *he* made," Violet pointed out.

"Master Snap," Holly said, turning back to the dragon, "I understand that your relationship with Sir Violet is strained. But helping us might not even require you to leave your home. And we will do our utmost to pay whatever price you name."

"I doubt that will be necessary. What is it you need of me, Holly?" the dragon asked.

"*If* you would be amenable . . . " she began, "Sir Violet told me that you possess an extraordinary sense of smell."

"Of course I do. I am a dragon."

"We were wondering if you would be able to recognise Juniper's scent from one of her belongings. Even if you can only point us in the direction she went, that would be tremendously helpful."

"You want to employ me as your sniffer dog," Snap concluded.

"I know it doesn't sound respectful," Holly said. "But I assure you, we mean no offence. All I want is to know that my wife is safe."

"You've heard a lot of stories where it was important to be polite to dragons, haven't you?" Snap smirked. "Violet must have missed those."

"I've never been rude!" Violet crossed his arms, decidedly not pouting, nor thinking of the fact that forgoing to ask someone's name in all that time didn't exactly make him a paragon of good manners.

"I *was* fond of dragon tales as a child," Holly admitted. "I kept asking my grandfather for new ones. I think he could have written a book, as he kept coming up with so many variations on the old themes. After spending all that time with fictional dragons, it is a great honour to meet you."

"I suppose there is some truth in those stories," Snap said. For a moment he tilted his head in thought, and then he nodded. "I will help you. I see no reason why I wouldn't."

"Thank you." Clearly relieved, Holly made to offer Snap the scarf, but he held up a claw.

"I don't need that, thank you. I have caught her smell."

Snap made for the cave's exit and, once outside, stretched like a cat—or, Violet estimated, like a pile of about seven hundred cats.

Then the dragon righted himself on his hind legs and sniffed the air, the crown of spikes behind his ears waving softly in the breeze.

"She must have started early, to get so far away," he said thoughtfully. "Unless she moves faster than Violet. It's been a while since I had the chance to compare human speeds."

"She'd been gone for some time when I came to see you, remember?" Violet said. "And you were all cranky because it *was* early."

"So where do we need to go?" Holly asked.

"Up into the mountains," Snap said, gazing towards the peaks in the northwest.

"What? Why would she go there?"

"I don't know," Snap replied, "but if you want, I can accompany you. There are many different paths, and you don't want to get lost. Travelling with me would make things easier."

"Please," Holly said. "That would be very generous of you."

"A generous thief. I don't think Violet thought he'd ever hear me described like that."

"Let's get moving," Violet suggested. "Where's the nearest path?"

Holly and Snap regarded him silently.

"What?"

"You want to walk there?" Snap asked.

"Well . . . Juniper must have done the same. Surely Willow would have told us if one of his horses were missing."

Snap spread out his enormous, black wings. "Don't you think flying will be faster?"

"You may not have noticed because we only ever meet inside your cave, but Holly and I can't fly."

"Good thing you know someone who can." Snap lowered himself to the ground. "Now please, climb onto my back before I change my mind."

"Oh." Violet stared at the dark scales, shining purple in the sunlight. "Are you sure?"

"Come on," Holly said, hoisting herself onto the dragon's back, behind the wing joints. Once she was safely seated, she held out a hand to Violet. "It's really our only option. We'd never catch up with Juniper on foot after half a day."

"I never thought I'd do this," Violet muttered,

but with Holly's help, he managed to sit down behind her.

He had thought he would be terrified. After a lifetime of having both feet firmly on the ground, flying had not sounded appealing at all. But secretly . . . it was amazing! He could see all of Ynys behind him, glimpsed what was beyond the other bank of the river, saw the fields shrink into a green and brown chequered carpet.

Even as they rose into the fog and he had to look over the side of Snap's wide back to see the jagged rock beneath them, he was quite certain that this was the best thing that had ever happened to him.

So of course the dragon had to ruin it.

"Please stay in the middle," he said. "It's exhausting to make adjustments for your weight all the time, and if you fall, I doubt Holly will appreciate the nosedive. That is, if we are in time to catch you at all."

"Point taken," Violet mumbled, centring himself once again. "It's just— You never told me how beautiful the world is, seen from the sky."

"You were walking on it," Snap said. "I thought you knew."

As Violet marvelled at the feeling of the cold air around his head and at the white landscape of ridges and crevasses to their sides, he almost forgot that they were on a quest. It might have taken almost an hour, but it felt far too soon when the dragon started his descent.

"Hold on tight," he warned, and Violet became aware that he liked this part a lot less.

Making the mistake of holding onto Holly's waist rather than clawing into Snap's scales, he almost dislodged them both as they finally made contact with the ground. Violet decided he might as well just let go and slide off completely, but hadn't taken into account that the dragon was not crouching and thus quite a bit higher up than he expected.

"Oof!" he cried as he landed on his back in the soft snow.

"Are you all right?" Holly asked, waiting until Snap lowered himself before elegantly leaping off.

"Fine!" Violet got to his feet and pretended to brush off the snow so they wouldn't notice he was actually rubbing his backside. "So . . . we're here, then?"

Snap squinted his eyes. "I suppose my landing was a little off the mark because I have to balance differently with you two on my back. But we must be close. Come along."

Violet and Holly sank to their shins into the snow as they waddled behind the dragon, Violet cursing the impeding weight of his sword.

Fortunately, the snow melted a little wherever Snap put down his paws or tail, so they soon found they were more comfortable following his track. This time, Violet did understand why Holly was snuggling deeper and deeper into the scarf.

Down in Ynys, it was spring. Here on the mountaintop it was freezing. Sitting on the dragon's warm back, too excited about flying to pay attention to his body, he hadn't really noticed. Now he dearly missed his winter coat.

He reluctantly picked up his pace so he'd be closer to Snap. Which, of course, meant he bumped into his tail when the dragon stopped suddenly.

Once again, he landed on his back in the snow.

"Sorry about that," Snap said. "I found it!"

"Oh, it's nothing," Violet answered as he scrambled upright again. "Who needs dry trousers when they're already freezing to death?"

Holly was looking at the ground between Snap's front paws. As Violet stood beside her, he saw a small, round, silver object in the snow.

"You think that a bell will lead us to Juniper?" Holly asked, puzzled.

"Oh. No, this has nothing to do with Juniper." The dragon frowned. "I understand why you might think so. But no. This just caught my eye as we flew over. It's smaller than I expected from the gleam, but look." He hooked the tip of a claw behind the ring at the top of the bell. "It's very pretty. And it smells only a little bit of sheep."

"Pretty?" Holly grabbed the bell and threw it as far away as she could. "You're telling me we're wasting time here because of such a ridiculous thing?"

"Hey!" Snap followed its flight with his eyes. "I was going to hoard that!"

"You can grow your hoard when Juniper and I are back home!" Holly took a deep, trembling breath. "Please. Until we've seen that she's safe, I want no more distractions. From you *or* Violet."

"Now what did *I* do?"

Snap's gaze lingered in the direction where the bell had flown and he looked sadder than Violet thought was possible for a dragon. But then he seemed to pull himself together. "Fine. I'll return for it later. We'll just hope no one else ever comes here to hoard things, right?"

He dropped to his belly and for a moment Violet thought it was his way of mourning the lost treasure, but then Holly climbed onto Snap's back and Violet realised he should do the same. Hopefully the warmth would dry his clothes a little faster.

Though Violet's time perception might have been altered by the way he was laughing with pleasure—and possibly lack of oxygen—high in the sky, it couldn't have been more than ten minutes before Snap landed again, on a mildly sloping surface covered by an even thicker layer of snow.

"What is it this time?" Holly asked, resigned. "A weathercock?"

Snap shook his head. "Juniper's scent is strong. She can't be far away."

"Does that mean humans smell really bad to you when they're nearby?" Violet asked, resisting the urge to sniff his own armpits.

"No. They just smell of human. Specific human.

You smell of Violet, and Holly smells of Holly." Snap paused and added: "Not the plants."

"You're being honest?" Holly asked, her teeth chattering. "This isn't your quest for the next shiny object?"

"I may be a dragon, but you can believe *some* of what I say." Snap sounded a little hurt. But as he looked at the way Holly had wrapped her arms around herself, his expression softened. "I suggest you stay here while I figure out where exactly Juniper has gone."

"I wish we could make a fire," Holly muttered, shivering.

"Seriously?" The dragon chuckled. "Do your brains freeze that easily?"

He took a step back and opened his mouth.

"What—" Violet started, but Snap didn't make to bite Holly as he had feared.

Instead, a weird bubbling noise sounded from Snap's stomach, and then a large ball of fire shot out of his mouth.

"What!" Violet squeaked.

Holly jumped back, but the fire landed neatly between Snap and the place where she had stood a moment before. Within seconds, it had sunk through the snow and melted a large circle around it, without any of the flames ever leaving the perfect orb shape.

Breathing in the cold air made Violet aware that his mouth hung open. And that he should probably move closer to the fire if he didn't want to freeze his bits off.

"You can't be surprised." Snap gave him a mocking look. "I'm a dragon. We breathe fire. Didn't your stories teach you as much?"

"Bu-but . . ." Violet said, and his stammer was definitely caused by the cold and not because he was impressed, "I never saw it happen. I thought maybe *you* couldn't do it. And I'd never pictured it like this."

"Well, here we are." Snap shrugged his folded wings. "Please get closer before you turn into an icicle. I assure you it's safe."

Holly and Violet cautiously approached the fireball and sighed almost at the same time. It was like stepping into a hot bath.

"I will be back soon," Snap promised.

They didn't really talk while they waited for the dragon, and Violet was grateful that he could simply enjoy the heat. He soon learned that moving as little as one step away made the freezing air bite at his back. He was standing closer to the ball than he'd ever dare with normal fire, though it seemed a bad idea to touch it with his fingers. He might have tried it anyway if Holly hadn't said: "Maybe don't. I have a feeling it might pop like a bubble, and then we don't want to be this close to it."

Snap had bits of snow on his wings when he returned down the slope. He was looking rather thoughtful as he joined them by the fire.

"Well?" Holly asked.

"I have good and bad news," he replied, and Violet ducked away so the water melting from the dragon's wings wouldn't drip on his head.

"The good news is that I am quite certain that I have found Juniper. The bad news is that, well . . . there is bad news."

"What do you mean?" Holly asked, looking alarmed.

"I think you better come and see for yourself."

Chapter Four

Violet frowned at the wooden sign. It was crooked, bending under the weight of snow piling behind and partly on top of it. The same pile that was stopping them from going any further up the slope.

"What use is that?" he wondered out loud. "Why would someone make a sign saying this is a way, but without mentioning where the way leads? Or are they telling us 'way to go' because we made it this far?"

"I think the real question is: who are *they*?" Holly said. "No one ever goes into the mountains. At least not from our side. And look at all the snow. This can't be one of the paths. So why is there a sign at all?"

"Actually, it *is* a path. Only, it was hidden by what I assume was an avalanche." Snap brushed some snow off the sign with his claws, and now it read:

DANGER! GO AWAY!

"Oh, that's reassuring," Violet remarked. "What exactly are we doing here?"

"Finding Juniper," Snap answered. "The trail clearly leads here."

Violet frowned and looked all the way up to the ridge of rock far above, then back at the untrodden white mass in front of them. "You think Juniper has turned into snow? Was it a wizard?"

"She is *under* the snow. Isn't she?" Holly's voice was soft and she had gone quite pale.

But rather than replying, Snap startled them both by letting out an enormous roar.

"Whoa!" Violet tentatively reached out a hand to the dragon's elbow. "Look, I know this is frustrating . . ."

"Ssh." Snap tilted his head and listened. "Yes," he said after several seconds. "I was right."

"About what?"

"There is a cave behind all this snow. And there has, indeed, been an avalanche."

"How do you know?"

"I could tell from the echoes that there is an opening in the rock behind the snow. I doubt a human could hear the difference, but to my kind, it is a great advantage to be able to find hidden caves.

As for the avalanche . . . If there were any snow left on that ridge above our heads, it surely would have come down after a loud noise like this. But everything has fallen already."

"What? You *tested* that while we were standing here?" Violet stared at him. "You're unbelievable!"

"I know," Snap said. "Now if you would please both get out of the way. I am about to create a river and have been told that drowning is not a recommendable death."

"So you think that Juniper is in the cave?" Holly asked hopefully, as they moved to the spot Snap indicated.

"Only one way to find out." And with another bubbling noise, Snap opened his mouth and breathed a fierce stream of fire at the mountainside. Water splashed over his paws, apparently hot enough to make the snow further down the slope melt too. Soon there was indeed a small river flowing down to where Violet and Holly had been waiting earlier.

An opening became visible at the top of what was left of the pile of snow, but Snap had to pause for breath before he could launch another stream of fire. After three more pauses, most of the pile was gone and an entrance wider than the one to Snap's own cave was free.

"Go . . . Go on in," the dragon panted, and Holly and Violet obliged, cautiously stepping around the puddles.

"Hey, guys!" a voice echoed through the cave. "I can see light! I think we can go out again!"

"Did you hear that?" Violet asked Holly, before crying out: "Hello! You have visitors!"

A sound like thunder rolled from the back of the cave and for a moment, Violet wondered if they were about to meet another dragon. However, as the rumbling approached, he was able to discern a jumble of running footsteps, and then Holly and Violet were surrounded by dozens of people, who were pointing rusty swords and spears at them.

"Oh dear," Snap said as he leisurely strolled into the cave after them. "Forgot about the sign, did you?"

A few people gasped at the sight of the dragon, but one of the men yelled: "Yes! You should have known better than to barge into our home! Our revenge will be sweet." He thrust his spear forwards a few times.

"That really didn't look as impressive as you

hoped," the young woman next to him remarked, keeping her own sword very steady. Another woman stood behind her with an arm wrapped around her waist and her chin resting on her shoulder, looking more like a happy cat than like a threat.

"We mean you no harm," Violet said loudly. "In fact, we have freed you." He gestured behind him at the entrance.

"*We?*" Snap huffed.

"Yeah, it *is* nice that we can go out again." The teenager, whose voice they'd heard echo through the cave earlier, lowered his sword, but quickly lifted it again when he saw the expression of the man beside him.

"You are unwelcome," that man said. "Intruders in our home. Leave, before you regret not doing so. Or . . ." He frowned. "Before you're no longer able to regret doing so?"

He looked back at the boy, who nodded. "That!"

"She is right," Snap said, pointing a claw at the girl with the snuggler glued to her back. "You guys are not impressive at all."

"Mean!" several people cried.

"We are looking for a woman who left our village earlier today," Violet said, hoping to get back to the point of their quest. "If you tell us where she is, we will leave you alone."

"We won't tell you where anyone is!" someone shouted.

"Not unless you become one of us." A woman around Violet's age smiled and winked. "I wouldn't mind sharing my space with you . . ."

Violet's eyes widened and he stepped aside, so Snap would be blocking her view of him.

"Oh, not interested?" He heard her laugh. "Maybe Rowan should give it a try. You might like him more."

"I doubt it," Violet muttered, trying to ignore the dragon, who'd turned to him with a big grin. Fortunately, something else caught Snap's eye over Violet's shoulder.

"Oh," the dragon breathed. "That is a *beautiful* dress."

The large, bearded axe-bearer who wore the flower pattern looked down and blushed. "You think so? I made it myself."

"And a very talented person you are," Snap said. "Might I ask your name?"

"Almond." The reply was accompanied by a giggle.

"Snap," Violet said, "you are *not* going to undress . . . them?"

"Him," Almond provided.

"Undress him for your hoard. You won't." Violet crossed his arms and tried to imitate Holly's sternest expression.

Almond looked confused. "Yeah, I'd rather not take it off, it's kind of cold . . ."

"No more hoarding before we've found Juniper," Holly agreed with a look of her own.

"Fine . . . Always spoiling the fun . . ." Sulking, Snap stepped away from Almond.

"Holly?" The familiar voice came from the back of the cave. "Holly, is that you?"

"Juniper!"

Holly pushed the man with the spear aside and ran to the narrow opening from which the baker's voice had sounded. They met each other halfway in a crushing hug.

"I'm so glad you're safe," Holly gasped, burying her face in Juniper's neck.

"Oh good," Violet commented with a smile. "Our work here is done."

"How did you find me?" Juniper asked after a moment, stepping back a little so she could look up at

Holly's face and wipe away her tears. Violet noticed she wasn't wearing her apron, but had donned thick trousers which seemed a lot better suited for walking in the snow than his own.

"The dragon tracked your scent," Holly answered. "Juniper, meet Snap."

Snap didn't need to push anyone aside as he crawled closer to them. The circle had fractured into little groups who were whispering together, and only a few were still holding up their weapons.

"Now I get it," he said solemnly as he looked upon Juniper.

"Get what?" Holly asked.

"Why she took priority over the silver bell," he said. "Lady Juniper . . . your hair is so *shiny*."

Holly slapped a palm over her eyes, and Juniper laughed. "Well, I don't only take care of Sir Violet's cinnamon addiction when I trade with the merchants. They bring some great hair products, too."

"Pitchforks!" Violet reminded the dragon, standing by his elbow. "You will *not* be hoarding humans."

"Oh, hush. Or I'll tell that woman from earlier that you like *her* hair."

"You wouldn't dare!"

Juniper was still laughing. "Now which of us was the married couple again?"

Holly lowered her hands and gently took Juniper's. "Are we okay? You aren't angry with me?"

"Why would I be angry?" Juniper asked.

"Well, I did lash out," Holly said. "And then you were gone . . ."

Juniper winced. "I made a mess, didn't I?"

"I was just worried . . ."

"Oh, Holly." Juniper pulled her closer and gave her a soft kiss. "I didn't leave because I was angry. I wasn't. You had every right to say the things you said. I'm so sorry I scared you."

"I'm aware it's none of my business," Violet said, "but why *did* you come all the way here, Juniper?"

Juniper frowned and looked down, not letting go of her wife's hands. "My love . . . I want to be there for you. To support you. And yesterday I realised that I should do better. That I *can* do better."

Holly shook her head. "I shouldn't have made you feel like—"

"No, you should," Juniper cut in, looking up at her. "It was inspiring. And I should have realised that an explanation of *why* Moss said things that hurt you wasn't what you needed right then. I'm sorry."

"I'm sorry too," Holly said. "I wish I'd given us a chance to talk."

"I knew we would talk eventually, my love," Juniper said earnestly. "You have absolutely nothing to apologise for. We just both needed a little more time. But then an idea hit me, and . . . I really should have left a note, or even better, woken you to explain what I was going to do. I've been thinking about that all the time in here. But right then, it seemed like such a good idea that I had to go and do it immediately. I got dressed, grabbed my rolling pin and left."

"Hold on. You brought a *rolling pin*?" Holly threw her hands up in exasperation. "I've married a walking cliché!"

"Hey, it's effective! In . . . some situations," Juniper said.

"Like making biscuits!" Holly crossed her arms. "So what *was* so urgent that you sneaked off in the night?"

"You had told me that you wished there was a way to send the world a message. To teach everyone to be more accepting. And suddenly I remembered a story I'd heard a few years ago. A legend about a spider who builds cobwebs strong enough to span miles, and whose threads can carry sound."

Almond gasped. "That's not a legend! That's true! Iris, tell them!"

An old woman stepped forward. "Back when our community here was still young, some of us travelled all the way down to the other side of the mountains. We'd had enough of the snow and the rock and hoped that we would find a more hospitable place to live. But all we found there was a grim, thick forest. Everywhere we looked, spiders were crawling, and it turned out that some of the larger ones could talk. They asked us if we had come to send a message.

"'No,' we said. 'We have come to find a new home.'

"Of course that didn't please the spiders. They became defensive and didn't let us pass. Finally we managed to explain that we didn't fancy living in their forest anyway. They told us that they were guards of Cleome, the extraordinary spider whom young Juniper just described. In the course of time, many had come to them to send their messages through her webs."

"But you didn't send any messages that first time, right?" Almond prompted.

"No," Iris said. "We only realised how we could use her services later on, back here. We'd been having long discussions about ways to protect ourselves. If people believed that we were as scary as those spiders, they would leave us in peace. We would always be safe. So we returned and employed the spiders' services to ensure that everyone knew how dangerous we were and that everyone should stay away from the mountains."

"It's quite subtle, really," Almond said. "Just a whisper, travelling from the forest over the mountains through many spiders' webs, which people catch without really noticing. But when someone hears their friends talking about coming this way, they warn them about the dangers and change their minds."

Juniper nodded. "That was the story Heath told me."

"Heath?" Iris repeated. "You mean he's returned to Ynys?"

"Must be about ten years now," Holly answered.

Iris frowned. "I'd never expected he'd go back. There's a reason why we are living here, you know. In a community as tight as that of Ynys, people are bound to feel it all the more when they don't fit in, for whatever reason. I was one of the first who decided to join a group that would travel the mountains, because our small village could not be all the world had to offer. But soon we found that it was a difficult journey and we decided to make a place for ourselves here. Just for a while, until we found something better. But then it turned out there was only the forest on the other side, so . . . we stayed. An ever-growing group of hermits, who could talk to each other without judgement. Our only rules are acceptance and openness."

"Heath told me he did feel accepted when he lived here," Juniper said. "But as he was learning more about himself, he started to feel like he should be able to reunite with his family and make a home in Ynys. He'd found ways to express what he needed to feel comfortable. And while he understood the importance of protecting your community here, he personally didn't like the idea of scaring away outsiders, even if it was only through whispered stories. So he returned and his brother, the miller, took him in. They both needed to adjust to each other's presence after such a long time, but I believe he is really happy now."

"I'm glad to hear that," Iris said.

"So . . . he told you you'd find the spider by coming here?" Holly asked Juniper.

"Well, I figured that if these people had met Cleome, they could give me directions to her. Heath told me about his journey many times, so I knew that this cave lay along the path that starts closest to the village, and it wasn't hard to find."

"I see." Holly studied her wife's face for a moment. "I wish you had asked me to come with you. I was so scared when Snap said you were trapped in here . . ."

"Well, actually it was better this way." Juniper shrugged. "If I had brought you along right away, we'd *both* have been stuck in here. You wouldn't have arrived with a dragon to get us out."

"At least we'd have been together! At least I wouldn't have had to worry about you so much."

Juniper looked down. "I'm really sorry. I suppose part of me really wants to impress you. To show you that I can be a hero for you. That I *would* do anything to make you feel that I'm on your side."

Holly wrapped her arms around Juniper and rested her cheek against her hair. "I'm sorry, too. I shouldn't have made you feel like that was necessary. You are always enough."

"But I could do *better*," Juniper said. "I want to

make up for hurting you the way I did. I want to talk to those spiders."

"I think it's a great idea, if they can really send messages like that," Holly said thoughtfully. "But I won't let you go alone. I want to make the rest of the journey with you."

"I can give you a ride to the forest," Snap offered. "That will definitely save you time."

Holly looked up gratefully. "That would be amazingly kind."

"Wait a second." Violet glanced from one to the other. "That means I have to go back to the village on foot?"

Snap frowned. "Unless you come with us. There's more than enough room on my back and by now, I think I've become used to the differences in ballast."

"But . . . We found Juniper. I thought we could go home!" Violet said desperately.

"Maybe you should wait here," the woman who'd flirted with him suggested. "They can pick you up on the way back. If you still want to go by then."

"Oh. That's . . . very . . . hospitable of you. But no. I've just realised . . . This will be a matter for which they need a knight."

Snap grinned. "Great! Though I must say I'd almost be tempted to stay myself. This is a very nice cave. Almost as nice as mine. You people have good taste."

The woman and some others laughed.

"Especially when the exit's free!" the boy, who had now left his sword leaning against the cave wall, said.

"But . . ." Holly gave Juniper a puzzled look. "Surely you can't have been in here long. You weren't riding a dragon, so if you had to cross that distance on foot . . . how can you already be on *this* side of an avalanche?"

"Oh. Yeah, I've only been here an hour or so. I actually sort of *caused* the avalanche," Juniper confessed, scrunching up her nose.

"What?"

"Well, she startled us," Almond said. "Oleander had seen movement outside, so they warned us. And we all came running out, screaming. Sorry for giving you such a scare, Juniper."

"Don't worry about it. The creaking and rumbling above my head was a lot more alarming," she replied. "The snow on the ridge began moving and we all ran in here as fast as we could.

Fortunately everyone made it. But I thought we'd be stuck for ages. I guess most of us did . . . There was a lot of consternation and I tried to help calm people down, but at the same time I couldn't stop thinking about you, Holly. Wishing there was a way to go back in time and talk to you, or at least leave you that note."

Holly nodded. "I'd still have come and found you."

"I know." Juniper smiled.

"But if you're going to travel all the way to the forest," Iris mused, "you better take some food. I don't know how fast the dragon flies, but it's quite a long way from here."

"So we do need to return to the village first," Violet said happily. "We didn't bring anything."

"Peony, can you pack some meat for them?" Iris asked the boy.

"Sure!" He disappeared in the passageway at the back.

"I'm just not sure it will be enough for a dragon," she told Snap apologetically.

"Oh, don't worry about me," the dragon said, crushing Violet's last flare of hope. "I'm good for a while. I ate only last month."

"But I understood that you never return to the village," Holly said to Iris, looking confused.

"No, we don't," she answered.

"Then how can you have provisions?"

"Oh, that. We keep sheep up here. Usually you see some of them around, but I guess they ran away because of the avalanche." She shrugged. "We'll find them again. It'll keep us busy for a couple of days. And in summer, when most of the snow has melted, we can grow vegetables."

"Do any of those sheep wear silver bells?" Snap asked, fascination clear in his voice.

"Yes," she answered. "Did you see them?"

"One of those bells, yes. I did wonder how it got there." The dragon studied Iris for a moment. "I don't suppose you have a spare?"

"Er . . . Of course," she answered, frowning. "Why do you need one?"

Snap lowered his large muzzle almost shyly. "I just like them."

Almond grinned proudly. "I make those, too! I was training as a smith before I came here."

"Wait, I remember you!" Violet realised. "Your family used to live in my house!"

"Really? They don't live there anymore?" Almond

smiled. "Guess Dad bought that farmhouse he was always dreaming about."

Violet nodded.

"That's nice to hear. At least one of his dreams came true, then. I ruined the other one. He wanted his son to become the best blacksmith of the village. But I always snuck out of the smithy to go watch what the seamstress was doing, and when I did stay, I preferred to work with delicate objects. Gold and silver jewellery rather than iron fences, that kind of thing." He looked around at the flirty woman. "Camellia, could you get a bell for our friend Snap?"

"On my way!"

Chapter Five

The bell's leather strap would fit comfortably around a sheep's neck, but couldn't even serve as a wristband to Snap. Almond extended it with two long ropes and once the trinket had been secured under Snap's chin, the dragon swung his head left and right several times to make it ring.

Peony also soon returned with a package of dried meat, and Juniper put it in her backpack, which had contained little more than her rolling pin before.

"It's a shame the stories never linger on practicalities," she mused as she hoisted it onto her back. "It would make it so much easier to go on an adventure if they did."

"Maybe they don't actually want to *encourage* us to go on adventures," Violet pointed out. "Considering that the heroes usually run into a lot of danger . . ."

"Or maybe long checklists would make the stories less exciting," Holly said with a smile.

"Everyone ready to go?" Snap asked.

"No," Violet muttered.

"Oh, come on. You of all people should feel good about this! Having an actual adventure will do wonders for your skills as a knight!"

"I've had an adventure coming here, thank you," Violet huffed. But he definitely didn't want to stay behind with the hermits, who all seemed to know each other so well. He'd feel more lost here than out in the wild, however nice these people might be. And especially if they were being *too* nice. So he trudged slowly towards the exit of the cave.

Juniper shrugged on her coat and gave Holly her hat. "Better not take off that scarf. It's pretty cold out there . . . "

"We noticed," Violet said grumpily. Even still inside, the draft made him cross his arms tightly over his chest to prevent himself from shivering.

"I was lucky Heath told me all about this place," Juniper said. "He often said that the temperature was what he loved most about Ynys. It seemed a silly thing to say on bleak autumn days, but now I think I understand what he meant."

"Be careful when you go out," Almond warned them. "The melted snow is freezing again. It won't be long until we have an ice slide."

"Really?" the two snuggling women said in unison. Grinning widely, they let go of each other and ran over to look.

Iris stepped forward and pressed Juniper's hand between her own. "Safe travels, and good luck," she said. "Give our love to the spiders."

Most of the hermits were waving at them as Violet, Holly, and Juniper took off on Snap's back. Even the two women, as they rushed down the slide with a loud: "Wheeee!"

Violet wanted to turn around and wave back, but he didn't have much room to move. At Holly and Juniper's request, he had sat down between them so he would be sheltered from the worst of the cold. He was grateful for it, too, as the dragon had lost a lot of his heat after breathing out so much fire. Yet he wished he could have seen the rock where the avalanche had started, to make sure that Snap had been right about there being no more snow. Or the way the people would grow smaller and smaller as the dragon beat his wings. With a shrug, he decided to enjoy the landscape before him instead.

They landed in the forest by nightfall. Violet had been excited when he caught the first glimpse of a mixture of broad-leaved and coniferous trees in the distance, not only because it had to mean they were nearly there, but also because it was marvellous to see the uneven, mottled green pillow of treetops from above. Even though he knew better, he imagined that if he were to fall off Snap's back, he'd land softly in a cloud of leaves.

"Come on," he said happily as he slid off Snap's back. "Let's find the spiders quickly, so we can get home before midnight."

Snap frowned. "I'm sorry. I don't think that's a good idea. We'd better set up camp now. I can smell many things, but not spiders. I have no clue how far into the forest we will need to go to find them. It might take hours, or even a day."

Violet's good mood crumbled very quickly,

but they all agreed to rest and Snap created a smaller fireball to keep them warm. It wasn't really necessary—in fact, the temperature seemed a little higher than it had been at home—but it was cosy all the same. They ate some of the meat, sitting on the soft earth, and discussed that none of them really knew how 'setting up camp' worked. Juniper said she had once spent a starry night in the fields near Ynys with a friend, but they had known that nothing dangerous roamed there, so a few blankets had been enough to get comfortable.

Here, they had no idea if anything or anyone more threatening than the spiders lived close by, and there was barely a surface large enough to stretch out on that wasn't overgrown with prickly small plants or bumpy tree roots.

"I will keep watch," Snap promised. "I don't need much sleep and I can see in the dark better than you."

Indeed, the thick foliage filtered out the light of the rising moon, and Juniper and Holly were no more than shadows to Violet by the time they lay down to sleep.

Violet decided he might as well follow their example, but although he lay a little distance away in order to find a more comfortable spot, he still heard them whispering to each other.

There was always *something* poking in his back or his ribs. He kept shifting and turning, and with every sigh he wished harder that he was back at home.

"Violet?" the dragon said softly. "Are you all right?"

"Of course," Violet replied, trying to keep still for a minute. Holly was now snoring softly, and he didn't want to disturb those who *could* find sleep.

"Are you sure?" Snap asked. "You seem uncomfortable."

"Of course I'm uncomfortable." Violet sighed again and sat up.

"Sit with me," Snap offered. "The night can be long and dull when you're on your own. You're probably regretting that we lured you into coming along."

"Not really," Violet confessed as he moved closer. "I do wish I had a mattress, though."

"So you don't regret that you didn't get to talk to Rowan? Or the lady who mentioned him?"

"No." Violet wrapped his arms around his knees, frowning. "I'm sure they were all very nice. That some of the people there could become my friends. But when they start a conversation with expectations like that . . . I just lose interest very fast." He shrugged.

"Oh," Snap said. "You lay watching Holly and Juniper for a while just now. I thought that perhaps you were jealous. Not of them, specifically, but . . . of what they share."

"No. Not in the way you might think, at least. I *am* a bit jealous that they're at ease anywhere, as long as the other is there too. It does make me feel lonely that I'm the only one here who isn't fit for . . . adventures. That the three of you don't really understand. I mean, that's not supposed to sound accusing. It's just the way it is."

Snap's smile was visible in the light of the fire. "Maybe I do understand. Maybe it only takes talking to me. If you choose to trust me, rather than to consider me the criminal who only sets out to cause you trouble . . . Well, I think we could be good friends."

Violet let out a mirthless laugh. "You're a dragon. You are comfortable everywhere. You're always confident and indestructible. How could you ever understand?"

"I am also, except for your visits to my cave, quite lonely."

Violet studied the large face, but couldn't see much of the dragon's expression. "I thought you chose to be alone. That you were like me."

"Like you?" Snap asked.

"I mean . . . I like the freedom of living on my own. The idea that I can go out at all hours if anyone needs my help or if I just feel like taking a walk, without waking anyone. Just having my own place where I don't need to worry about anything. I never feel lonely there. I can choose to go out and meet friends, and maybe it would surprise you, but I have a lot of them. And I love them. But if I had to be around any one of them all the time, I would be exhausted. And I think I would start feeling like this. Like there's no reason for me to be around and keep them up with my complaining at night."

"Of course there's a reason for you to be here," Snap protested. "Just like there is a reason why I steal more things than I would ever consider adding to my hoard. I like your company. You're the closest thing I have to a friend."

"Really?" Violet raised his eyebrows. "Even

when I only ever visit you to scold you and take away parts of your hoard?"

"At least you visit," Snap replied.

Violet felt an uncomfortable stab of pity. "If it means that much to you, why did you keep luring me into your lair by inconveniencing others? You could have *asked* me to come over now and then. Or moved into the village, so you could meet more people."

"Violet, I am a dragon," Snap said. "I couldn't ever move into Ynys. The reason why there haven't been any pitchforks, as you like to put it, is that I am distant enough not to be considered a threat. I don't take up anyone's space. But if they felt like I did, how peaceful do you think my life would remain?"

"I suppose you have a point," Violet replied, though he wondered silently if it couldn't be arranged. If, after all this time, the council member whom he had once convinced that Snap wouldn't cause any harm still thought that a dragon in the village meant danger rather than protection. "You could still have asked me."

"I'm not that brave. Stealing was a certain way to bring you to the cave. But if you *told* me you'd rather not be there, there would be no way back."

"You dragons use some very twisted reasoning," Violet remarked.

"I don't know if it's a general feature of our kind, or just me." The dragon smiled a little sadly.

"I think I'd still have come. If I hadn't thought I was only there to reclaim items you didn't really want to return, I might even have asked your name."

Snap laughed. "Now let's not exaggerate."

Violet chuckled and sat quietly for a while. He'd always thought of the dragon as a part of his work. The creature stole things; he would go to retrieve them. They'd rarely talked about anything else. Only now did Violet realise that it had been wrong to assume that Snap wouldn't *want* to get to know him better, just because he was a dragon. "So . . . if you want to be friends, does that mean I can ask things I've been wondering about?"

"Of course," Snap said. "We can talk as much as you want."

"Okay." Violet hesitated, then asked: "Had you been living in the cave for a long time before you stole the mayor's chain?"

"Oh. No. A few weeks at most," Snap answered. "I can't quite remember, but I know that I smelled riches from the very first time I flew over the village, and that was when I knew I wanted to find a place nearby. And it actually took some plotting to get my claws on that chain. I've always loved a challenging theft."

"I still wonder how you ever got a wedding dress out of a wardrobe," Violet admitted.

"Oh yes." Snap's teeth gleamed in the firelight as he grinned. "That was a very good one."

"Where did you live before?" Violet asked.

The grin disappeared. "Well, it's funny. You think I'm comfortable anywhere. There was a time when I didn't even know what the word meant." Snap snorted. "I grew up in a desert. It was magnificent. The golden plains were like a sparkling treasure as far as the eye could see. Had I been a desert dragon with golden scales that reflect the sunlight, I probably couldn't have been happier. But my kin originates from the mountains, where we seek out chilly caves. I absorb the heat and turn it into fire, rather than the ice with which the desert dragons cool and hydrate themselves. I was constantly burning both inside and out, my skin was irritated by the coarse sand getting everywhere, and there was barely a sip of water to be found. I assume my parent had left the egg there because it would hatch without any effort in the sunlight. Growing up, I didn't know better than to be alone. But I was terribly anxious."

"I'm so sorry," Violet said. "They just . . . They just *left* you there?"

"Yes." Snap sighed. "We dragons don't like each other much as a rule. Most parents do stay with their young long enough for the egg to hatch and the hatchling's wings to dry, but I imagine my egg-parent decided that leaving me somewhere warm was a quicker solution."

"Did you go looking for them?" Violet asked.

"No." Snap shrugged. "At that point I wasn't really aware I should have had a family. I was home, because the desert was the only place I'd ever seen. How was I supposed to know that anything else existed? I admired the scintillating sand and collected desert roses."

Violet was quiet for a moment, taking it all in. Then he asked: "What happened to make you realise you could leave?"

Snap's gaze focused on a point far away among the tree stems. "One day, for the first time in my life, I had visitors. Two humans who were huffing and puffing in the heat, pieces of cloth tied over their heads to protect them. I thought it was a part of their bodies. That the bags over their shoulders were their wings. I'd never heard of clothing or of people. But they were walking in my territory. My only instinct was to chase them away."

"Did you kill them?" Violet asked.

"I don't think the thought occurred to me at all. I only wanted them to be gone. To *stay* away. At that point, I might have been too scared to go close enough to touch, let alone harm." Snap frowned. "It must have been terrible for them. They were parched and exhausted, and I made them run for miles. Finally we came to the border of what I considered *my* desert. I'd never given it any thought why, but there was a small gathering of houses, so I suppose my distrust of other living creatures had kept me away all that time.

"I let them go then, and returned to my nest, feeling very good about myself. I had shown them. I was the master of this desert, and no one could take that away from me."

"And yet you didn't stay," Violet said.

"No. When I returned, I found that two of my favourite desert roses had disappeared. They were the only things I had managed to hoard there. They aren't plants, but structures of crystals in the sand. I haven't seen them in years, but I think I would still appreciate their beauty. However, at that time, I only cared that they were *mine*.

"Somehow, before I had even noticed that those humans were there, they must have stolen them. I turned around immediately and flew all the way back to the houses. But of course they were no longer there, waiting for me to attack them and claim back my prizes. I circled the village several times, but I caught no trace of them between the other screaming and crying people. And so I moved on, further away from the desert.

"Ahead, I saw something in the sky, and at first I thought it was a bird. Those sometimes travelled over the desert, but seldom landed, and so they had never really bothered me. But then I saw that the shape was wrong. There was a flat surface and on top of it the figures of two humans, sitting down.

"Later, I learned that I had been chasing a flying carpet. Its magic made it rush from me at a speed I could barely keep up with, and they had quite a head start. But I never gave up. Beneath me, the landscape changed. It was no longer the red and yellow of the desert, but there was blue of water and green of plants. I never halted to appreciate it. My only goal, my only thought, was to catch them.

"The sun set and rose again, and I had a feeling that we had travelled halfway across the world by the next evening. I was so tired that I hardly noticed we were descending. The carpet landed in front of a cottage surrounded by trees. And so I landed too, but I was too exhausted to attack. I just stared at the pair and they looked back at me, until they finally decided they dared to move. The man stayed, never breaking eye contact, while the woman went indoors. She returned with a bucket of water and set it down in front of me. And waited.

"Even I was thirsty after a journey like that. But I did not drink.

"She stepped closer, and closer, and when her hand landed on my back, I was too startled to snap. I kept as still as I could, and she petted my scales. Her hand was cool and soft and small, and there wasn't any scalding sand scratching at my skin.

"When she stopped, I followed her hand without thinking and she laughed. Somehow I knew that it wasn't some aggressive cry. Somehow I was starting to trust her.

"Eventually I drank the water, and when they

fed me, I ate. The man, too, petted me, and he introduced himself and his wife as Thistle and Acacia. I said nothing, but I stayed, wishing so badly to be petted and talked to that I had forgotten all about the desert roses.

"The next day, I did remember their theft, but they were still kind and I decided that I was in no hurry to leave. The air was fresh, both moss and grass were more pleasant to roll in than sand, and the small brook running behind the cottage contained enough water to make it splash when I hit it with my paws. They let me experiment, watching fondly or carrying on with their own business, and by evening I felt very strange. It was like energy was racing through my veins, like I could easily take another flight like the one the day before, except that I did not want to move away from this place. I was *happy*.

"I decided to stay one day more, a week, a month. In the end, Acacia and Thistle cared for me all their lives. They were alchemists, studying the properties of the elements. They'd lived in the desert when they were young, but their research had brought them to many different places, and finally they'd settled there, where they taught others their skills and could trade knowledge and metals. They showed me how they pulverised only a small portion of one of the desert roses' leaves and left the rest intact. They demonstrated how they could turn it into gold. *Real* gold—not some optical illusion." Snap licked his lips. "It was the best thing I had ever smelled. The shine entranced me and it felt so fresh and smooth against my skin. And yet I did not want them to do the same to the rest of the roses. I still believed that I might carry them home one day.

"They respected my wish. There were other ways to obtain gold and sometimes I would help them do business with faraway places, if the load was too large to carry on the carpet.

"When Thistle died, I was twice as old as I had been when I left the desert. Acacia and I were both heartbroken, even though he had become an old man, and humans cannot be expected to live as long as dragons. I stayed with her, of course. Together we still found some small joys, found that the memory of him brought smiles more often than tears. And then she passed away, too." The dragon was silent for a while.

"I'm sorry," Violet whispered.

"It was centuries ago," Snap said, staring into

the fire. "Centuries, and I still love every memory of them." He cleared his throat. "Their home was the safest place I had ever known, but I couldn't stay there on my own. Every single thing would remind me how much I missed them, and I couldn't bear the pain. But I also finally accepted that I would not return to the desert. I left the desert roses on their graves and took off, without a destination. I only knew I wanted to go somewhere where humans lived. Because these two extraordinary beings had taught me more than I ever thought I needed to know. They had shown me that there were places that suited me better than the one I came from, and more importantly, they had taught me how it felt to be loved."

"But if you wanted to be around a large number of people, why did you come to live near Ynys?" Violet asked.

Snap smiled. "Unfortunately, I found that not all humans were like Acacia and Thistle. In most places, I was attacked just for passing by. It saddened me, but I couldn't blame them. I'd been the same, after all. I too chased and almost hurt people because I was afraid. So I fled from place to place, hoping for a quiet life somewhere. And sometimes I found it.

Like now. In Ynys. Your people never attacked me. They accepted my presence and even my hoarding. And then *you* came into my cave and you were not afraid or hostile. You treated me as an equal and you visited often. It was the closest I had come to befriending another human. Of course it couldn't be compared with the couple. But if it was the best I could get, I could live with that."

Violet sat back a little, staring at the dragon. "But . . . you said it had been centuries. And you *never* had another human friend?"

"Nor any other," Snap said, tilting his head a little. "There was this bat once, with whom I shared a cave. He was nice, but then again he never talked much."

"And other dragons?" Violet asked.

"Well, as most of them probably *do* feel the need to stay and defend themselves when they are harassed by humans, I imagine there aren't many left. I met two of them, but as I said, we are a territorial species. Even if we can't avoid contact, we are generally glad to see the back of each other."

Violet sat in silence for a long while, processing the story. He was honoured that the dragon had opened up to him. But he wished more than ever that he had at least bothered to introduce himself properly all those years ago. The fact that Snap had not *expected* kindness didn't mean he'd deserved how awful Violet had been to him.

"I threatened you with pitchforks," he mumbled. "After all you've been through."

Snap laughed. "You were upset about Juniper. If I *had* harmed her, you would have had a reason to come after me."

"But . . ."

"I'm fine. We're good," Snap promised. "It all happened a long time ago. I became better at avoiding aggression. Just . . . Sometimes I was too tempted to find company to heed the risks."

Violet nodded slowly. Even if the thefts could be terribly annoying sometimes, he'd definitely do his best to be nicer to the dragon in the future.

Chapter Six

Violet woke up slowly. He was vaguely aware that the birds were noisier than other mornings, and when he wanted to hide his face in his pillow, it didn't give way. It also didn't feel soft, but smooth and leathery. And warm. Frowning, he struggled to sit up, but his spine was very stiff.

And then he realised. He had been leaning against the dragon. He'd been sleeping with his head against Snap's side.

Mortified, he checked the dragon's face, hoping this had gone unnoticed, but of course Snap was awake. Violet was about to say sorry, but then he noticed a gleam of joy in Snap's eyes. A smile that reminded Violet of the happier times in Snap's story. So instead, he muttered: "Thank you." And then ostensibly busied himself with finding some breakfast in Juniper's bag.

Even by day, the forest was only dimly lit. The further they went, the denser the trees grew, driving Holly, Juniper, and Violet to walk close to each other. Snap often had to find little detours in order to fit between the wide trunks.

"Are you okay?" Violet asked after the dragon had struggled his way through a gap with a horrible scratching noise as his scales grated against the coarse bark.

"I'm fine," he growled, reaching a paw to his ribs to assess the damage.

"Wouldn't it be more comfortable for you to fly?" Juniper asked. "You could go ahead and tell us how far we have to go."

"I won't see any spiders through those leaves."

"Yeah. Just stay down here," Violet agreed, looking around. He had a feeling someone was spying on them from the bushes, and without a dragon by their side, it would get a lot harder to stay calm.

"Look at that. It's beautiful!" Holly pointed ahead at a tree that stood a little apart, where sunlight could actually reach it. A large cobweb was spun between its branches and the dew drops covering it shone like stars.

From that point on they began to notice more and more cobwebs, of increasing size.

"We must be close now," Juniper said. And then she stopped walking. "Very close . . ."

Several cobwebs, as high as Holly was tall, hung between a row of thick trees. Violet stepped forward, frowning as he laid a hand on the hilt of his sword.

"I don't think it's a good idea to cut through those," Snap warned. "The spiders probably mean to keep us out of this part of the woods."

"But . . ." Violet took another step, and suddenly Snap let out a shriek.

Out of the tree closest to the dragon, a mass of spiders rained down. They landed on the giant creature, covering his scales in a coat of brown.

"Snap!" Holly cried.

"Dohon't wohohorry," Snap said, shaking his body wildly left and right in a way that did nothing to ease Violet's mind, and made the bell around his neck clang loudly. "It juhust tickles! Enough!"

Dozens of spiders fell to the ground as Snap

pried them off with his tail, but more and more of them were crawling down from the trees as well. The largest ones came to Violet's knee and soon neither he nor Holly and Juniper could move.

"Let us pass!" Juniper shouted, pulling the rolling pin from her backpack in a swift motion and swinging it against one of the spiders. Violet watched the arachnid fly through the air, come down, and shake itself before once again joining the others. Then he remembered that he had a weapon too and drew his sword, pointing it at the spider in front of him.

"Don't!" Holly exclaimed.

The spiders made their jaws click more loudly.

"Please, leave them alone!" Holly said. "Remember that we want their help. Hurting them will only mean trouble."

"They seem keen enough on hurting *us*." Violet recoiled and bumped into another spider behind him. "Sorry," he mumbled as an afterthought.

Snap was still distracted by shaking off the smaller spiders.

"Could you hold still?" Holly asked him. "So we can explain to them what we want?"

"*Still?*" the dragon repeated, giggling madly.

"You try that when a thousand little legs run over your ribs!"

"So you want something from us?" one of the spiders surrounding Holly lisped.

"We would like to see Cleome!" Juniper tightened her grip on the pin as more curious spiders approached Holly.

"Why did you bring a dragon?" another spider hissed.

"We don't like these dragons," yet another murmured.

"We despise the fire that they carry!"

"We cannot let the dragon enter our realm."

The hisses and whispers grew in volume and Violet wondered if, when he'd thought he'd heard the leaves rustle before, it had really been the spiders talking.

"I mean no hahaharm!" Snap cried, panting. "Please, have mehercy."

"He's just our friend," Holly said. "He brought us here."

"And unlike you guys, he wouldn't hurt a fly," Violet added, feeling rather proud of himself, until he saw Juniper roll her eyes.

"What do you want from Queen Cleome?" the spider with the lisp asked.

"We want to send a message," Juniper answered. "The hermits . . . They told us to give you their best. They explained where we could find you and said you were their friends."

"Distant friends, then," a smaller spider mused. "They barely ever visit. Acquaintances, really."

"And they never met Queen Cleome herself," another said.

"We can pass the message on to her. There is no need for you or that dragon to enter our realm."

"But it's not . . . just one message," Juniper said. "There is more. There are stories that need to be told. Stories that are as important as her own legend. I think we *should* meet her ourselves."

Violet frowned, wondering if she meant the words, or if it was just a trick to make the spiders give in. He supposed they *would* have a more spectacular tale to tell at home if they could describe Cleome, but he wasn't sure he wanted Juniper to press the matter. The spiders were annoyed with them already, and the next stage of their defences would probably be more deadly than a tickle war.

It didn't sound like she would convince them, anyway. The spiders kept clicking and hissing, and they were still standing uncomfortably close. If the ones behind him decided to bite, there was nothing he could do about it.

"If we consider the hermits our friends," the spider with the lisp said finally, "it is because they do not bring dragons. Because they are polite and leave our forest when we ask them to."

"Of course," Juniper said, casting her eyes down. "We're sorry. And . . . I'm sorry about hitting you."

"They are humans," Snap told the spiders with a shrug. There were still a few brown spots crawling over his back, but at least he seemed to have caught his breath. "Their kind is easily frightened, and it makes them lash out."

"Yes." The largest spider rubbed its legs together in thought as it studied Juniper. "You do look honest. Like *you*, at least, believe that your stories are worth telling."

Juniper and Holly both nodded.

"If we choose to let you pass, you will not touch any of our webs. You will follow the path we show, and not take one step out of line. You will not waste Queen Cleome's time, and we will warn you that if you even think of doing anything that violates her safety, we will not hesitate to let you experience exactly how venomous and sharp our fangs are. Is that clear?"

"Yes." Holly swallowed.

More spiders turned to Juniper, waiting for her answer, and then to Violet and Snap.

"Knowing these conditions, do you still want us to take you to her?" the spider asked then.

"Yes," they all said, though Violet's reply was almost inaudible.

"Then come along."

Three spiders worked together to unhook one side of the web from the tree, allowing the humans and Snap to enter without damaging their gate.

Violet's company was tense and silent as they followed their hosts. The spider realm didn't look very different from the rest of the forest. There were only more spiders.

After walking for at least an hour, they once again stopped in front of a large web. Here, however, the trees that held it up didn't stand in a neat row like they had seen before, but instead were scattered in all directions, making the web look like an angular . . . palace, Violet realised. This had to be Cleome's home.

"My Queen," one of the spiders said, though Violet couldn't see to whom, "these visitors begged us to let them see you. They claim it is important."

"Who are they?" a pleasant voice rang from above them.

With a hairy leg, the spider nudged Holly's shin to make her talk.

"I am Holly, and this is my wife, Juniper, and our knight, Sir Violet. We have come all the way from Ynys with Snap's help."

"A dragon," the reply came from above them. "You don't see many of them these days. I sometimes marvel at them not calling in my help to search for others of their kind. Don't they worry about the continuation of their species?"

Snap winced. "We live very long lives. I think, for now, there are enough of us left."

"Yes. For now . . ."

From a treetop a spider descended, slightly smaller than most of the ones on the ground. The other spiders all clicked their jaws, and only when

Violet wondered if this could be Cleome, he realised that they were saying the word 'Queen' over and over.

She was not what he had expected. Somehow, he had pictured her the size of a dragon and utterly terrifying, but in fact she looked less scary than the others. The angle of her many eyes seemed kinder, rounder, like a soft smile rather than a threatening grin. Or perhaps it was the lightness of her voice that made her more charming.

"Pray tell me," she said, "what *did* bring you to my lair?"

Holly and Juniper glanced at each other before Juniper nodded and directed herself to Cleome.

"We wish to make use of your webs. If you're willing, we would like you to build one that spans the whole world."

"You may underestimate how large the world really is." Cleome narrowed all eight of her eyes as she frowned. "I have never woven anything over such an enormous distance. It might take years and I would need to retrace my footsteps many times to be certain it remains secure."

"I understand that it would be a lot of work," Juniper said, "but I think it would be worth it."

"Why?" the spider asked. "What message do you think is so important that everyone should hear it?"

"The message that being different from what is considered the norm does not mean you will lead an unhappy life."

"We would collect as many stories as we can, from all over the world," Holly added. "Stories that prove that we do not need to be protected from our identities. That sticking with the expectations people have formed about us since birth is not the key to happiness. That if people are accepting, many problems can be solved. Stories like that of me and Juniper." She smiled at her wife. "But also many different ones. About different communities, different orientations, different characters."

"And not just that," Juniper said. "The web could be used to spread so much knowledge. To teach people about subjects that only inspire fear in them because they don't know their true nature. And, on the other hand, to warn them of the real dangers. If it ran everywhere, one village could wire another when they spot bandits. I imagine it would be faster than sending a courier and it would definitely reach more people at once."

"There is wisdom in that idea," Cleome said slowly. "But it would be expensive."

Juniper hesitated. "We have some money. And we own a bakery in Ynys."

"What would I do with a bakery?"

"Ask that again when you've tasted their cinnamon rolls!" Violet piped up. "Once you've tried them, you'll never want anything else. Juniper could provide you with food for the rest of your life."

The spider laughed. "I'm afraid, Sir, that our tastes are not similar."

"Well, I guess she could make them with a filling of flies instead . . ." Violet scrunched up his nose.

"Perhaps I can help," Snap said, and everyone turned to look at him. "I own a considerable hoard of valuable items. Surely I possess some objects that are of interest to you."

"And you wouldn't mind?" Holly asked incredulously. "I mean, that collection must have taken years to build. There isn't really any profit for you in this."

"If there is one thing that I have learned in my long life," Snap replied, "it is that there are always more pretty things to find. I would gladly donate it all to your cause. In fact, it would be nice to start anew. I would no longer be thinking about what fits in with what I already have, and thus discover new fields. So if it helps, you can have it all, until the last coin and the last silk dress."

"Silk?" Cleome repeated, righting herself in her web. "Now you do have my interest. I do not so much ask for riches, for here in the forest there is little we can buy with gold and silver. But to span the world, I would need more silk than I could ever produce myself. Even if it is not made by spiders, but still of high quality, I can connect it so that it will carry the sound just as well as my own. It would be a tremendous help, and a beautiful price to pay."

"So we get you as much silk as you need, *and* gold to buy more," Snap decided. "I do admit it will pain me to see some of my nicer pieces being reduced to threads, but I will make sure that their designs are not forgotten. I presume that Violet here could introduce me to a tailor who can draw and document the clothing for the future."

"Certainly," Violet said. "As long as they've forgiven you for everything you nicked."

"But why?" Juniper asked Snap. "If this is your life's work, how can you just give it away?"

The dragon smiled at her. "Humans live such short lives compared to mine. They cannot travel the world for decades, looking for an accepting home. What you are proposing will, hopefully, teach many people to accept others much faster. And when your story reaches people like yourself, it will let them know that they are not alone. It will remind them, even in dark moments, that they deserve love and people who love them for who they are. When their friends and family hear the story, they will be reassured that their loved one will be fine, and that differences are nothing to be afraid of. Stories like that can prevent so much pain and loneliness in those limited lifespans. How could I not support that?"

The women both stood watching him for a long moment. Then they rushed towards him and wrapped their arms around his neck.

"Yes, all right, okay," he muttered, his yellow eyes looking a little moist as he tried and failed to hide his giant head in the hug.

Violet patted his elbow with a chuckle. "I think you may have found yourself some more friends."

As Holly, Juniper, and Snap discussed with Cleome how they would make their project work, Violet sat waiting on a spider-free rock. Although he'd really only been tagging along, he felt proud. He might even have to admit that the dragon was right. Maybe adventures *were* good for him. Just one night in the wild and he'd gotten to know Snap better than after ten years of going through the same motions every time he visited. And he was glad to be part of what Holly and Juniper had started. Not only because he hoped they would achieve the results they aimed for, but also because as they talked, he had realised how nice it would be if, once in a while, the bard would come to the pub and tell a story with characters like him. Where the happy ending would not involve a man and a woman riding off into the sunset together, but someone who ends up at home, wrapped in a blanket, sipping a cup of hot milk and eating a pastry.

It was odd, really. They had all these tales about rare creatures like dragons, which had taught him all about them before he'd even met Snap. And yet he'd never heard a single one about a girl whose identity did not match the way her body was perceived by others. Not until he was old enough for the gossip about Holly to reach him, and now, recently, as she in turn had told him about Lilac.

"Ready to go home?" Juniper interrupted his thoughts cheerily as she, Holly, and Snap returned to him.

"If there is no more that needs doing, yes," he answered.

"Oh, there is much more to be done," Holly said. "We'll need to talk to a lot of people to collect enough stories to make a point."

"Now *that* sounds like an exciting new hoard." Snap's eyes twinkled.

"An exciting new quest, definitely," Juniper agreed.

Holly took her hand. "I still wish you hadn't given me such a fright by running off, but . . . I can't thank you enough for this. For thinking of a way that we can make a difference, and not just in Ynys."

"That's what I'm for, isn't it?" Juniper shrugged. "To support you in good and bad times. With brilliant ideas and tasty recipes. Or wasn't that what our vows said?" She tilted her head and narrowed her eyes in mock thought.

Holly playfully hit her arm. "Hush. But promise me one thing."

"Of course." Juniper grinned.

"Please let me join you on your next quest. Take me with you."

"Of course," Juniper repeated, and kissed her lips. "I couldn't do it without you."

Chapter Seven

Violet sighed in relief as Ynys came into view. He could have an even better look now that they were flying towards it, and he became particularly excited when he spotted the roof of his own house. Of course it would be there, next to the smithy and across the seamstress' shop, but this unusual perspective gave his home a magical glow. He couldn't wait to go in and close the door behind him.

However, Snap landed in the square a couple of streets away from it, facing the bakery. It was late in the afternoon and quite a crowd had formed out there. Some people were looking uneasy, never having seen the dragon up close, but Violet was pleased that they simply moved out of the way without too much fuss.

"So there you are!" the miller called out. "I came to bring you your order of flour, but there was no one here to accept it!"

"And no cakes on my little Oak's birthday," the shoemaker said, putting her hands on her hips. "I really hadn't thought the bakery would be closed for *two* days. If I'd known, I'd have ordered something from Bluebell's!"

"Sorry," Holly said, sliding off Snap's back and holding a hand out to Juniper. "There was a personal situation."

"We'll open again tomorrow," Juniper promised as she stood next to her wife. "I'll work through the night and make sure we have everything you need."

"Even cinnamon rolls?" Violet asked hopefully, still sitting on the dragon's back.

"Of course." Holly laughed and helped him down, too.

"But," Juniper said to the crowd, "you will have to accept that from now on, the bakery will no longer be open every day. We will announce exactly when we're closing and for how long, so that you can prepare for our absence, but Holly and I will be devoting some of our time to travelling."

There were frowns and some unintelligible, malcontent muttering.

"No wonder Violet was in such a state when you went missing," Snap said, amused. "Those cinnamon rolls must be quite something if people can't go a day without them."

"They *are*," Violet said, and Juniper nodded.

"I'd love to try them sometime." Snap licked his teeth.

"Well, come over tomorrow and that can be arranged." Juniper grinned. "I might even give you one for free."

"Ooh, in *that* case I will consider it." Snap winked.

"But they will have to learn to survive without them," Holly mused, looking on as the crowd dwindled. "Of course, we won't have to collect all the stories ourselves. Once the web is in place, everyone will be able to add to it. But first they'll have to be aware that it's there. Or at least that it's being built. Someone has to tell them . . ."

Snap nodded. "Fortunately, the world is not quite as large a place for a dragon as it is for a spinning spider. When you're at work, I can travel and spread the word for you. I was planning to search for more extraordinary fabrics anyway. And you can also send notes with the boats when they pass."

"All wonderful ideas," Juniper said, reaching up and scratching him behind his left ear. Snap froze in surprise, but then leaned in and purred.

When Violet entered the bakery the following morning, Snap was nowhere to be seen. He really shouldn't have expected the dragon to be there so early, he thought with a smile.

"Good morning!" Holly greeted him cheerfully, already picking up his treat.

"Thanks," Violet said, putting a coin on the counter.

The bell tinkled behind him, but the sound was almost drowned out by an ear-splitting: "Auntie Holly!!!!"

A child in a white dress threw herself full force into Holly's arms.

"Sorry about that," Moss said, laughing nervously as she closed the door. "We came to visit you yesterday afternoon, but you weren't home. And Lily really, really wanted to see you, so I promised we'd come back first thing in the morning. Guess she took that literally."

Holly stared at her with the six-year-old lifted in her arms.

"I wanted to show you my dress!" Lily squeaked. "My *own* dress, Auntie! Mummy made it for me!"

"It's . . . It's lovely," Holly stammered.

"And, and, and, she says it's fine if I want people to call me Lily! It really is a pretty name, don't you think, Auntie?"

"Beautiful," Holly agreed, looking dazed.

Moss smiled a little sheepishly. "Thanks. For talking to me . . . And sorry for running every bad scenario by you. I forgot to pause and think how it must have sounded."

Holly nodded. "I . . . I think it's okay now."

"That's good to hear." Moss bit her lip. "It's just . . . Your advice matters more than that of my neighbours or any of the people who've deemed it necessary to give me their opinion. You actually know what you're talking about. But I shouldn't have sprung it all on you without warning."

Holly tilted her head in acknowledgement. "No . . . but it's all right now. I think we both just want the best for Lily, so . . . Please know that you are welcome to keep talking with me. That you can both come to me anytime you want and that I'll try to help you in any way I can." She put Lily down, taking a step back to look at her. "It really is a nice dress. Suits you perfectly."

"Thank you!" Lily did a happy twirl and beamed at her mother.

Moss nodded, tears shining in her eyes, and walked around the counter to pull Holly into a hug. "Thank you."

"What's all this? Do I hear a little Lily skipping around the bakery?" Juniper asked, laughing as she came from the back. She hugged Lily and then joined Moss and Holly's embrace.

"Good morning, indeed," Violet said, smiling. Touched by his friends' happiness, he hadn't even taken a bite of his cinnamon roll yet. Now he felt he should give them some space, and with a nod at Juniper and Lily—the only ones who were looking—he went outside.

Snap sat waiting in the square, the sheep's bell jingling as he turned his head towards Violet.

"I trust all is well in there?" he asked.

"Very well," Violet answered, tearing his cinnamon roll in half. "Here you go."

The pastry looked tiny between Snap's claws and he sniffed it carefully before he put it in his mouth and growled in pleasure. "You didn't exaggerate."

The DRAGON of YNYS

"No." Violet silently ate his own half, and then said: "I've been thinking."

"And you didn't invite me as a witness this time?" Snap teased. "I'm hurt!"

Violet poked his leg. "I guess you shouldn't worry. I wasn't really thinking. I was *wondering*. About what I am supposed to do now."

"What do you mean?"

"Well, if you're off travelling, hardly anything will get stolen here, will it? Hardly anyone will need to employ a knight anymore."

"Ah." Snap smiled. "Remember that my hoard will decrease greatly. I will need to rebuild my collection when I *am* home."

"Well, that's a relief," Violet said, rolling his eyes. "The thing is . . . I wonder if I couldn't do anything more useful."

"One night at home, and now you do crave the adventure?"

"No," Violet said quickly. "I love being home. But I also love . . . I love helping out."

Snap studied him for a long moment. "I suppose you could keep me company," he said then. "As you postulated, there won't be any thieves when I'm away. You might have time to spare. But obviously you shouldn't feel obliged. If you don't want to leave Ynys at all . . . Though we could return often. I have grown rather fond of this place, so I would in fact like to."

"Yes," Violet said, and Snap's eyes lit up. "When do we leave?"

The dragon laughed with delight. "Well, not yet. I still have to sort out which of my items will be of use to Cleome. But you can help with that, too."

"One condition," Violet said, and Snap tilted his head. "You're flying me to the cave. I won't be walking."

The dragon chuckled. "Deal."

The bakcry's bell rang, and Moss and Lily walked over to them.

"Whoa! Violet, is this your dragon?" Lily looked up at the creature in awe.

"No." Violet smiled up at Snap. "He's ours. Snap, the mighty dragon of Ynys."

Lily grinned and held out a hand. "Nice to meet you, Snap!"

Snap shook it so carefully that it would not break even if it had been made of spider silk.

Epilogue

There was a problem.

The hermits had been rather disappointed when they realised that it would get too cold in the mountains for the web. The threads would freeze and, unable to vibrate, they couldn't carry any sound waves. So, from the beginning of winter all the way until the thaw, the cave residents wouldn't be able to receive the contents of the web.

Fortunately, the solution was relatively simple. Many of the stories that would circulate the web came from the books Snap had begun to collect. The spiders entered them into the web themselves, and although Violet had been sceptical about that—imagining the hissing and clicking he'd heard when first visiting their realm—their reading voices were in fact very pleasant to listen to. Apparently, the objectionable noises had merely been a sign of alarm.

Snap had decided that once the spiders were finished with the books, he might as well store them in the hermits' cave. That way, even when the webs were frozen, those who lived in the mountains would still have access to stories.

The decision wouldn't have surprised Violet quite as much if Snap had actually been able to enter the hall where they were now building the hermits' library. As it was, there was no way the giant dragon could fit himself through the narrow opening leading from the entrance cave further into the mountain. The cavern extended into a whole network of tunnels and smaller grottos in which the inhabitants slept, all around the central hall where the carpenter was now hard at work to make rows and rows of bookcases.

However, Snap didn't seem to mind at all. He'd flown Violet and Master Spruce to the hermits' cave every day for a week now, and on the days he didn't fly off to gather more books—Violet had resolved not to wonder whether they'd all been lawfully acquired—Snap would simply lie down and chat with the hermits until Violet and Spruce wanted to go sleep in their own beds in Ynys.

When Violet asked, the dragon explained that

he didn't need to see the bookcases for himself to know the hoard was there. He was more concerned with protecting the beautiful covers from snow and dirt, which wouldn't be quite as easy in the entrance cave.

While the cave residents had seemed wary of the carpenter at first, communicating mainly through Violet, they'd warmed to him after a couple of days and now there were enough helping hands to take over whenever either of them needed a break. As Violet walked to the entrance cave, still catching his breath from lifting a too-heavy wooden plank, Snap was talking about Ynys with Peony and Periwinkle, teenage siblings who'd been born here in the mountains and had never been to the village themselves. Snap had been spending a lot of time in Ynys lately, though he still lived in his own cave, where he was free to occupy all the space he needed and the risk of being woken too early in the morning was much smaller.

Violet was about to join in and invite the youths to come along and try Juniper's pastries, when he saw Camellia approach. He halted and almost fled back to the central hall.

"Master Snap," Camellia said, "I wanted to ask you something. I've always thought that being a librarian sounds like fun, and now we actually *have* a library. I do trust that everyone will treat the books with respect, but wouldn't it be reassuring if someone took care of the shelving and made sure everyone can find the stories more easily?"

Snap gave it some thought. "It would," he replied. "If none of your neighbours object, I wouldn't mind assigning you Head Librarian."

"Camellia would be great at that!" Periwinkle enthused. "She's really organised."

"Thanks, Periwinkle." Camellia smiled. "I'll discuss it with everyone at the cave-meeting tonight."

Violet still stood dithering a little distance away. If he was honest with himself, he hadn't expected that Camellia would be the type to take on a large responsibility like that. And he wouldn't be able to avoid the Head Librarian forever when he accompanied Snap on book deliveries, so it would probably be best if he followed her example and acted responsibly as well, rather than handling his discomfort by running away.

He took a few steps forward. "Camellia," he said hesitantly, "can I speak with you?"

Camellia turned away from the dragon to look at him. "Sure, darling."

Violet winced. "Yeah, about that, actually."

"Oh." She blinked and followed Violet into a tunnel where they could continue their conversation more privately. "You don't like being called 'darling'?"

"Well . . . I wouldn't mind if it's someone who calls *everyone* darling . . . But when we first met, it felt like you were making advances to me, and . . . I'm not interested in any of that."

Camellia regarded him contemplatively. "I'm sorry for upsetting you. I wanted to make you feel a little more welcome and that was the only way I could think of. Everyone else was pointing spears and other sharp things at you . . . "

"That was also uncomfortable," Violet conceded, "but it felt less personal. And I'd rather not avoid talking to you forever, but I also don't want to give you the wrong idea. A romance or any of the things you might have implied just isn't for me. I mean, *some* activities sound appealing, like a picnic in the moonlight or a candlelit dinner. I suppose they're generally considered romantic, but I can just as well share them with friends. I don't want any of that with one person in particular."

"I understand," Camellia said. "In fact, I read about someone like you in one of the books that have been added to the web. The writer called herself aromantic. I can look for it if you want to borrow it."

"That would be great." Intrigued by the new word, Violet decided to give it more thought once they were finished talking.

"So . . . no soppy endearments for you," Camellia summarised. "It's almost a shame. I could have come up with some really original ones."

"You still can if you like." Violet shrugged. "I mean, I don't mind, as long as I'm not expected to be anything other than your friend."

"Right." Camellia grinned. "Careful what you wish for, sugarfluff."

Violet snorted in amusement and made a point of exaggerating his grimace.

"Too much?" She actually looked concerned.

"No, not at all. It's funny." Violet smiled. "Let's see how long you can keep up that challenge."

"All right, pumpkin." She blew him a kiss. He caught it from the air and threw it over his shoulder.

As they both laughed, he felt a lot lighter.

In the early evening, Peony and Periwinkle accompanied Violet and Master Spruce on Snap's back. Going by their delighted gasps, the sight of the houses alone already satisfied some of their curiosity about Ynys.

When they landed, the bakery was still open. Holly and Juniper had placed some tables and chairs in the square, where a story could be heard loud and clear from the thick cobwebs covering the bakery's front wall. A group of children had been sitting together to listen, but as soon as they saw the dragon and his passengers, they ran over to greet them.

"Master Snap!" Lily squealed. "Can you tell us the story again about the hero-princess and the witch who was sometimes a girl and sometimes a boy?"

"And sometimes neither," Snap added with a smile. "Of course."

After exchanging a curious expression, Peony and Periwinkle joined the children as they all gathered around the dragon. Violet considered sitting down with them—it *was* a good story—but he was feeling a little worn. He walked around the tables into the bakery.

"Cinnamon roll?" Holly asked with a knowing smile, even though it was far too late for breakfast or even lunch.

"Yes, please. You're a gem. And do you have any pastries left for Peony and Periwinkle to try?"

He brought an apple turnover, a honey flapjack, a walnut swirl, and a plate of sweet kringles over to the children and waved at Snap as he walked away with his own cinnamon roll.

Once home, he prepared a cup of hot milk, wrapped himself in a blanket and, humming happily, enjoyed the sweet delicacy. When he'd licked the last crumbs off his fingers, he opened the book Camellia had lent him and started reading.

The END

Afterword

The Dragon of Tnys was first published in May 2018 by Less Than Three Press (LT3). When I found their open call for submissions near the end of 2016, my first short story had only just been published in the *Unburied Fables* anthology, and I was dreaming about my next step: writing a fairy tale long enough to be a book on its own. The dragon-themed call prompted me to expand on a story that had been brewing inside me for a long time. It had started in 2011 as a short tale written in my first language, Dutch, about a knight and a dragon who didn't really see any point in fighting each other and became friends instead.

LT3 was the first LGBTQIA+ publisher I had discovered. The fact that the book *needed* queer characters for them to accept it made me realise that I could write the kind of story that I would personally enjoy and it could still be *published*.

It would become a light, fun fantasy tale for all ages—because I wished I could have read its messages of acceptance when I was much younger, but I would also enjoy this type of tale now, in my late twenties. A happy story full of elements that bring me joy, like baked goods and bad puns and—obviously—dragons. A story with trans, lesbian, aromantic, and asexual representation. (Let me just clarify that Violet and I happen to be both aromantic and asexual, but of course many people who don't experience sexual attraction *do* experience romantic attraction, and vice versa!)

I was delighted that, once the book was out, several people described it as a warm hug. A safe place.

And yet, it turned out that wasn't true for everyone. I will always be grateful to the reviewer who respectfully pointed out how the first version of *The Dragon of Ynys* contained elements that were hurtful to trans (both binary and non-binary) readers. Parts of the story of Holly, Juniper, Moss, and Lily were, in hindsight, clearly tinged by some of the internalised transphobia I carried. Even when we do our best to be accepting, we are sometimes marked by the things we've heard throughout our lives, and that can make it harder to accept ourselves than it is to accept others.

By (to some extent) denying my own identity, I hadn't given Lily the support she deserved. It turned out that Moss, Lily's mother, had been telling the child not to be trans much more loudly than I ever realised while writing or editing the 2018 edition of the book. In addition, it appeared that the cis characters—even though they were trying to be good allies—were drowning out the trans characters' voices. Of course I had never intended for any of that to happen; it went against the entire point of the story! But it *could* be interpreted that way, and it did hurt readers. For that, I apologise profusely.

In July 2019, I received the sad news that LT3 was going out of business. I will always think of this publishing house with fondness, as they amplified the voices of people who are all too often unheard. They allowed our stories to take flight in a way that offered many advantages to both writers and readers. If they hadn't believed in *The Dragon of Ynys*, this story would probably be gathering dust somewhere, mostly forgotten, and it's possible I might not have been motivated to write as many short stories as I have in the meantime. So, from the bottom of my heart, I am grateful to them.

While the shock of their sad message hit me and many others in the queer community, the rights to *The Dragon of Ynys* were reverted to me, and I had to ask myself an important question: "Now what?"

The review that had made me realise the problems of my story had never left my thoughts. I felt I owed it to the readers to work on those issues before republication.

It was a longer process than I had foreseen. It really required me to take a closer look at why I had written certain words in the belief that they would sound supportive—and as I mentioned above, I hadn't been ready to write some of the scenes concerning Lily and Holly in 2017. I was still telling myself—more loudly than I realised—that the gender I'd been assigned at birth had to be "good enough". After all, it did feel right *sometimes*, didn't it?

It wasn't until after the first publication of *The Dragon of Ynys* that I openly identified as genderqueer. And I've learned now that, as a writer, you can't decide to accept everyone except yourself. By trying to do that, I ended up hurting people who are *like me*: readers who might have had high expectations. By now, I've learned that the more we give ourselves the chance to explore who we are, the better our stories will become—both the ones we write and the ones we create for ourselves in life.

At this point, I am exploring the labels "genderqueer" and "genderfluid", but going by my earlier experiences when I was figuring out that I am asexual and aromantic, it can take me quite some time to find a way to describe myself that feels completely *right*. Either way, it feels good to acknowledge that I sometimes feel more masculine and sometimes more feminine, and that about half the time I feel like no gender properly fits me, and to accept that about myself. It certainly helped me understand what I could do better in this book.

The second mistake I had made was that I had echoed some of the things I had heard from people who were trying to be supportive. Whose intentions were good, but whose knowledge failed them. The problem wasn't so much that I'd included those lines, but mainly that I hadn't properly challenged them in the text.

From the very beginning, it had been important to me that the characters in *The Dragon of Ynys* weren't perfect. That they all made mistakes, but that there would always be a way to set things right. Unfortunately, I hadn't made it entirely clear in my writing why the characters would never for a minute doubt that the others had good intentions, even when their words seemed to imply something else. I hope I've been able to fix that writing error without taking away from the characters' obvious, perhaps relatable flaws.

All of the characters—be it human, dragon, or spider—are simply trying to be the best they can be. Just like all of us. Sometimes the support we offer is not the support the other person needs. Other times, someone close to you may have absolutely no clue how to comfort you, but you still feel grateful because that person is there for you, and you couldn't possibly tell them how they could help you better, because you've never experienced this situation before, either.

Throughout this tale, the characters all learn that in order to be their best selves, they need to listen to others' stories. They need to learn to communicate, asking the person they want to help what they actually *need*. But they also need representation in stories, so that they can read about certain situations in life, see how the characters deal with it, and learn from it. After all, representation is not just about seeing *yourself* in a story. It also, more generally, opens our minds and explains the perspectives of other people around us.

And since this book was supposed to hold a helpful message, that means that to some extent, the characters did need to be a good example and communicate better than they did in the original version.

It's sort of fitting that I needed to revise those particular elements. After all, the book was always meant to show that making a mistake doesn't make you a bad person as long as you work to right your wrongs. You will always keep learning and do better in the future.

So that is what I've tried to do in this revision, with the help of the amazing E.D.E. Bell and our wonderful group of beta and sensitivity readers. I couldn't be happier with Atthis Arts' editing process.

Even though the book still contains heavy subjects, I hope I have done a better job with the way the characters deal with them. This is the story I needed, in more than one way. I'm glad that this journey—or let's also call it a quest!—has taught me so much.

I hope you enjoyed *The Dragon of Ynys*!

All the best,
Minerva
July 2020

Acknowledgements

Thanks to my parents, for making it possible for me to chase my dreams; to L.S., for saving both me and the plot, many times; to Tessa, Ava, Ether, Fie, and Jessi, for their support, sheep, kittens, and pumpkin seeds; to my "children and grandchildren" at HPO, for whom I first created Sir Violet.

Thanks to the team at LT3, for giving this story a chance in the world, to Samantha, Megan and Sasha, to Kirby Crow, to Leta Hutchins and V.E. Duncan.

Thanks to the lovely people who hosted blog tours and wrote reviews so potential readers could find out this book existed.

Major thanks to the Atthis Arts team for giving this Dragon new wings.

Major thanks to Emily, who is an amazing editor and will think of everything. E took the revision to the next level, which was exactly what I hoped for.

Thanks to Chris for the beautiful interior design.

Thanks to Gwynn for coming up with that perfect word that unfortunately none of us can remember anymore. It's somewhere in here and it's great!

Thanks to Ulla Thynell for the absolutely magical cover.

Thanks to my wonderful beta readers: Tessa, Ether, Ava, L.S., and Fie, who found flaws in logic and language that had gone unseen before.

Thanks to the wonderful sensitivity reviewers: Donnie Martino, Jasre' Ellis, Leda Scurrell, and consultants, for your valuable insights and guidance. The spiders would approve of how your perspectives on the story made it more secure and beautiful.

And thanks to you, dear reader, for choosing to read this story.

About the Author

Minerva Cerridwen is a genderqueer aromantic asexual writer and pharmacist from Belgium. She enjoys baking, drawing and handlettering.

Since 2013 she has been writing for Paranatellonta, a project combining photography and flash fiction. Her first published work was the queer fairy tale 'Match Sticks' in the *Unburied Fables* anthology (2016). Her short stories have also appeared in Atthis Arts anthologies *Five Minutes at Hotel Stormcove* (2019) and *Community of Magic Pens* (2020).

For updates on her newest projects, visit her website or follow her on Twitter.

minervacerridwen.wordpress.com

twitter.com/minerva_cerr

Lightning Source UK Ltd.
Milton Keynes UK
UKHW010647190123
415610UK00007B/783